DRAW ON DUSTY . . . IF YOU'RE READY TO DIE

The youngster came to his hands and knees. He shook his head and, through the roaring pain that fogged his brain, saw the Colt lying on the ground. He dived forward, scooping the gun up and rolling over to come to his knees with it in his hand. Someone yelled a warning, which brought Dusty spinning around. Dusty saw his danger and acted on it, his left hand leaping across his body to the white-handled butt of the Colt in his right holster.

All his life Frank Holman had wanted to see a real fast man in action. Right in front of him was the fastest of them all, but he never knew it. Half a second after Dusty's left hand started to move, Frank Holman was dead.

THE
FASTEST GUN
IN TEXAS

J.T. EDSON

A DELL BOOK

Published by
Dell Publishing
a division of
Bantam Doubleday Dell
Publishing Group, Inc.
666 Fifth Avenue
New York, New York 10103

Originally published in Great Britain
by Brown Watson, Ltd.

ISBN: 0-440-20818-1

Reprinted by arrangement with the author

Printed in the United States of America

January 1991

10 9 8 7 6 5 4 3 2 1
RAD

PART ONE
THE FUTILITY OF WAR

CHAPTER ONE

Sitting his horse on the south bank of the Moshogen River, First Lieutenant Cogshill listened with distaste to his commanding officer making a patriotic speech to explain to the company of New Hampstead Volunteers why they must guard the bridge behind them. Being a professional soldier, if a young and unblooded one, Cogshill knew the value of the bridge. It offered the only place in many miles where heavy traffic could cross the wide, fast-flowing Moshogen River. The old Corn Road ran down the northern slope of the Moshogen Valley, crossed the bridge, and rose up the southern incline. Apart from a small wood about a hundred yards from the bridge on the northern bank, the land lay open and without cover for attackers. Major Buller flatly refused to take the time to search the woods, despite the fact that his company arrived to take over their command some fifteen minutes after the old guard had departed, claiming that the river lay well inside Union-controlled territory, where no reb dared come.

Listening to his commanding officer, Cogshill cursed the fate that brought the Buller brothers into the Union Army. True, they equipped their own regiment, but he suspected that business interests and not loyalty to the Union dictated the move. A commission in the Union Army opened doors that would otherwise have been closed to the Bullers, rich as they were. However, neither of the Bullers had ever seen action, and the major did not realize the dangers of his lax regard for duty. The woods lay, like the Moshogen River, in Union-held country, but Dixie's colonels, Turner Ashby and

John Singleton Mosby, or Captain Dusty Fog, never allowed a small detail like that to worry them when they wished to raid a Union objective. Being aware of the South's raiding skill, Cogshill knew his men should be preparing their position, not lined up listening to a speech.

One of the listening troopers chanced to look upward and saw the rim above him lined with mounted men. Being a rookie, the man did not at first give a thought to the fact that the horsemen on the rim wore uniforms of cadet gray instead of Union blue. A full ten seconds after the first glance the difference struck him.

"Up there!" yelled the volunteer, his voice squeaky with excitement. "It's them rebs!"

Instantly the difference between Buller and Cogshill became obvious. While Cogshill opened his mouth ready to give orders, Buller sat and stared up the slope. A cold chill of anxiety hit the major as he found himself face-to-face with the men whom he often boasted he would rout in battle. Words would not leave Buller's lips.

Even before Cogshill could give an order, the tall, freckle-faced lieutenant in command of the Confederate force snapped an order. Showing riding skill far beyond that of the Volunteers, the gray-clad riders swept down the slope.

Watching the charge, Cogshill felt certain his men could not hold the bridge. The rebel cavalry appeared to be veterans, and each man drew a brace of 1860 army Colts; the finest handgun yet made. Against the Colts, Cogshill's men must depend on Pettingill, Joslyn, Manhattan, or Metropolitan revolvers; and the Volunteers had received little training in the use of their weapons.

Before Cogshill could give his orders, Buller took command. Jerking the ornate-looking navy Colt from his holster, he turned his horse toward the attackers.

"Shoot them!" he screamed in a panic-filled voice. "Get them!"

Both Buller and his burly sergeant-major, Packard, jerked out their revolvers and opened fire, but the rebels were still beyond any range where either man might hope for anything but a lucky hit.

Following their leaders' example, the troopers also started shooting, then found difficulty in controlling their horses. Yet it seemed that their resistance worked, for suddenly the rebels were fleeing back the way they came. Cogshill could hardly believe his eyes, but Buller felt sure that his theories about Confederate cowardice had been true.

"Get after them!" he yelled wildly. "Chase them!"

Memories of a lecture on Indian fighting tactics came to Cogshill, especially the thought of an old Kiowa trick, as he watched the flight of the rebels. Before he could warn his superior, Cogshill saw Buller start to race his horse up the slope. Next moment the entire company followed on its commander's heel, in more of a wild rush than an organized charge, the men firing off their revolvers indiscriminately. Duty insisted that Cogshill stay with his command and leave the vital bridge behind to follow the fleeing men. Fleeing? To Cogshill's eyes, the rebels held together remarkably well for a scared, running mob.

Topping the rim, Cogshill looked back in a purely instinctive gesture. What he saw made him bring his horse to a halt, leave his command, forget his duty to his commanding officer. What he saw was of more importance than even trying to save the half-trained Volunteers from the folly their leader was taking them into. So instead of turning and following his misguided, half-trained commanding officer, he started his horse down the slope again.

Captain Dustine Edward Marsden Fog, Troop C, Texas Light Cavalry, and his sergeant-major, Billy Jack, stood hidden in the shelter of the woods on the north bank of the Moshogen River and watched the arrival of the new guard. They stood, hands covering the muzzles of their big black horses, preventing any sound that might give warning of their presence. When the troop passed on, the two Texans moved toward the edge of the woods and the banks of the river. They moved in silence and were able to hear all that was said.

They made a contrasting pair, the two Confederate soldiers. Billy Jack was a tall, gangling, lean man with a long, miserable, sorrow-filled face, which hid humor and intelligence and a fund of the best dirty stories in Texas. His kepi was thrust back from his close-cropped black hair, his face tanned oak-brown by the elements. His prominent Adam's apple forced itself out of his open tunic neck. The tunic was well cut, and on the sleeves were the three bars and arc of silk that denoted his rank. Around his lean middle was a gunbelt with matched army Colts in the holsters, the bottoms of the holsters pigging-thonged to his legs.

Captain Dusty Fog was not a tall man, standing not more than five-foot-six in his Jefferson boots, although there was a width to his shoulders, a tapering down at the waist, and a growing, maturing strength about him that many a taller man might have envied. His build was emphasized by the uniform he wore, and for a man so strong on discipline Dusty was breaking a few Confederate Army dress regulations. True, the tunic had the prescribed two rows of buttons, seven in a row, four inches wide at the top, three at the bottom, as laid down in the regulations. The stand-up collar, sleeve cuffs, and stripe down the legs of his tight-fitting breeches were of the correct cavalry yellow. But the collar was open, and instead of the official black cravat around his throat he wore a scarlet silk bandana, the ends hanging long over his tunic. The flouting of regulations did not end there. His tunic was without the skirt extending to between hip and knee, but was cut off level with the top of his breeches. Around his waist was a *buscadero* gunbelt, and butt forward in the holsters were a brace of bone-handled army Colts. On his sleeves was the the elaborate double-gold-thread insignia of his rank, extending from the wrist to the bend of the elbow. On his collar, Confederate uniforms being without epaulets, were three one-inch-long, half-inch-wide gold bars.

His campaign hat was thrust back from his dirty-blond hair, and the face it exposed to the sun was young, handsome, strong, and intelligent. It was a man's face, and the gray eyes were even, firm in the look. The mouth was firm and strong, but it was a mouth that would smile easily, and there was nothing of the rank-conscious braggart about Dusty Fog. It was a face that showed strength, a face matured beyond its years by the harsh realities of war.

A man matures fast in time of war. So it was in the case of Dusty Fog. He and his cousin, the red-head commanding his waiting troop, Red Blaze, left their home at fifteen to follow their uncle, Ole Devil Hardin, into the Confederate Army. At sixteen Dusty was a first lieutenant, his seventeenth birthday brought him his third collar bar, and he'd served in that rank with distinction for the past nine months. He'd gained each promotion through cold bravery, skill, and ability, there was no man in the Texas Light Cavalry who could deny that.

"Thought that boy lootenant was going to make it real awkward, Cap'n Dusty," remarked Billy Jack. "I hopes young Red remembers his part of it."

"He will," Dusty drawled, his voice easy, not loud, and with a Southern inflection. "Don't you sell young Red short. He's steady enough when the shooting starts. Is that keg ready?"

"Fused and ready," replied Billy Jack, turning on his heel and lifting a small keg of gunpowder from the ground.

The barrel of powder lay on a pile of slashed tarpaulin, the covers wrapped around it to make it waterproof when Dusty and Billy Jack swam the Moshogen River in the cold light just before dawn, bringing their horses over and hiding in the woods. Dusty had almost taken a chance to blow up the bridge when it lay unguarded for those few minutes, but did not get the time. He could not believe that any soldier would be so foolish as to leave a vital bridge like this undefended for any length of time. Suspecting a trick of some kind, he waited and missed a good chance to wreck the bridge and get away without trouble.

Once more Billy Jack examined the keg, checking that no water could possibly have seeped through and spoiled the explosive charge. All was well, the keg dry and untouched by the Moshogen's cold waters. Billy Jack shivered at the thought of the waters. It was no fun swimming the river in the early morning, naked, with his clothes and gunbelt wrapped in a slicker. Now he hoped Red Blaze would remember Dusty's carefully given orders when the time came. He watched the crossing of the bridge and was puzzled by the lining up instead of getting down to the serious business of putting out pickets and preparing the guard.

Dusty held no such worries about his cousin's ability to handle things. He knew Red better than did any other person, including Red himself. To most people Red came into contact with he appeared to be a wild, recklessly brave young man and not long on self-control. Red was the sort of man who could not stand and watch a fight without pitching in on the side that needed help the most, without finding out who was in the right of the fight. But—and here was the thing that Dusty knew and other people were apt to miss— once in the fight, Red was cool, calm, and capable.

Red's present duty was to charge down the slope, then, when resisted, to run and draw the defenders after him. The Southern intelligence system knew which regiment was guarding the bridge, and this helped Dusty form his plan. He would have planned differently if faced by regular soldiers. Red was only to force home his attack if the men did not follow him up the slope. If they did not, he was to return and make a serious, determined attack, holding them down while Dusty and Billy Jack moved in on the other side and blew up the bridge.

Having heard Buller's unmilitary yells instead of orders, and watched the undisciplined rush after Red's party, Dusty knew he had called the play correctly. He doubted if the plan would have worked had the young Yankee lieutenant been in command. From the start, that shavetail had shown a good grasp of the situation and had given Dusty a few bad moments when he had suggested searching the woods. Fortunately the major overruled the idea and so played into Dusty's hands.

"Let's go," said Dusty, moving forward. "I'll get down on one of the supports in the middle and set the charge."

"Be the best place for it," agreed Billy Jack, watching Red's charge, then the retreat and pursuit. He was not surprised that Dusty's plan was working; it would have surprised Billy Jack if the plan had not worked. Even as they moved forward to the bridge, their horses following them, Billy Jack found himself comparing the cool and competent

8

way Dusty always acted with the wild way that Yankee major was carrying on. There would have been none of that wild, irresponsible action and those unmilitary yells instead of commands had Dusty been commanding the bridge's defense.

Dusty and Billy Jack went on to the bridge and walked along until they were roughly in the middle. There was a fast-moving yet unflurried way of working about them that formed a contrast with the way the Union troops carried on, a purpose to their actions that told they were well used to dangerous situations such as this.

Leaving his horse standing like a statue in the center of the bridge, Dusty went to the side and looked over. The bridge supports would be easy climbing—they were meant to be—allowing inspection of the underside and the hidden timbers of the supports. He swung over the rail and lowered himself down onto the nearest cross brace, bending to look underneath. The thick support he stood on was joined by a crossbar wide enough to take the keg of gunpowder, and this would be where Dusty would place the explosive charge. There was no time to spare in selecting a better place, and the charge would do all that was necessary on this spot.

Billy Jack lowered the powder keg to Dusty, then turned to watch the Union troops. Dusty wedged the keg into place as firmly as he could, both to make sure it did not jar loose and to compress the explosion, get more results from it. He took the slow match fuse and backed off to the edge of the support again, gauging the distance to the water and making sure the burning end of the fuse would not reach it when released. Taking a match from his pocket, Dusty rasped it against a timber and lit the fuse, watching to make sure it burned correctly.

"That young lootenant's seen us!" Billy Jack said in his usual bored voice. "He looks like he's going to be a hero."

"I'm finished down here!" Dusty snapped back. "Mount up and light out."

Billy Jack did not wait for second orders. He saw Dusty climbing back onto the bridge and went afork his horse heading for the southern side of the Moshogen River. Dusty remained long enough to see that the vibrations of the horse did not jar loose the keg. It was as he expected: The bridge was too stoutly built for one galloping horse to make any effect on it.

Swinging over the guardrail, Dusty ran for his big black horse and went into the saddle in a flying mount. The black lunged forward as soon as Dusty hit the saddle, racing for the southern shore, where Billy Jack waited.

A bullet whistled between the two men as they came together. Cogshill was coming back, riding recklessly down the slope to try to save the bridge. The young Union officer tried to get more speed out of his horse, and his revolver spat again, the bullet coming close.

Billy Jack flashed Dusty a grin that showed his admiration for the spunky Yankee lieutenant. It was only at such times that the hangdog left the lean soldier and showed him for what he really was: a bone-tough Texas fighting man.

"Be a real pity to have to kill that boy," he remarked as a third shot came close to hitting him. "He's getting to call his shots better all the time."

Dusty's eyes were watching Cogshill as the two came toward each other, gauging the distance and setting his arm up. His right hand crossed his body, and the white-handled army Colt slid from the left holster in a flickering blur of movement. The gun cracked and kicked up against his palm as the horses hurled at each other. Cogshill was lifting his gun for a more careful shot when something that felt like a red-hot iron smashed into his left shoulder. The force of the sudden blow and the intense pain of it made Cogshill drop his gun and slammed him back in his saddle. He managed to cling on and tried to draw his saber with his good hand as he closed with the two Texans.

The three horses hurled toward each other; it appeared that they must collide. At the last moment Dusty reined to Coghill's left, and Billy Jack went to his right. Unable to get his saber clear, Cogshill made a wide grab at Dusty, trying to pull the small Texan from his horse. The grabbing hands missed, for Dusty swung sideways, hanging over the flank of his horse. He'd been set to shoot Cogshill down but held his fire. He could not bring himself to kill so brave and keen a young man, even if the same young man was an enemy and might try to kill him the next time they met. Billy Jack's Colt was in his hand, but he did not shoot. He knew that had Dusty wanted it, the Yankee would be dead now. With this thought in mind Billy Jack lifted his revolver and slammed the barrel down onto Cogshill's head. Sick with pain and almost ready to collapse, Cogshill slid from the saddle and crashed to the ground. The two Texans rode by him, and Dusty turned to look back and make sure Cogshill fell free of his horse and was not being dragged. Then Dusty gave his full attention to the top of the slope. Ahead of him, over the top of the rim, came the sound of shots.

Major Buller's gallant charge took his men over the top of the rim. On the level ground at the top of the Moshogen Valley he urged his men on after the wild, fleeing rebels. Waving his gun, he exhorted his hard-riding troop to greater efforts, cheering them on in their pursuit of the running enemy.

Then the rebels weren't running anymore. One word from Red Blaze brought the troop wheeling in a tight turn and hurling back at the amazed Volunteers. Only this time they made their charge with guns in hand. The wild rebel war yell rang out, and the men of Troop C, Texas Light Cavalry, charged the New Hampstead Volunteers, shooting as they came. There was a difference in the shooting. Where the Volunteers were unskilled and shot wildly, these gray-clad riders were very skilled and sent their bullets with some precision. They did no wild shooting, sent no bullets harmlessly into the air, just fired fast and accurately.

Buller was shocked at this reverse of procedure. In the wild rush he remembered one rule he'd learned in listening to soldiers talk. The best way to dissuade an enemy was to shoot down the leader. He saw the young red-haired rebel lieutenant coming at him and lined his ornate-butted navy Colt. It was unfortunate for Buller that Red Blaze had also learned that same rule, learned it well and acted on it with both speed and skill.

The long-barreled army Colt in Red's right hand barked, flame-lanced from the muzzle, licking out toward Buller. The wind caused by the fast-running horses whipped away the black powder smoke, and Red could see everything clearly. He saw Major Buller rock back as the .44 bullet hit him. The man still clung to his saddle and Red came closer, then fired again. A blue-edged hole appeared in the center of Buller's forehead; then, even as a trickle of blood oozed from the hole, Buller slid down from his horse and crashed into the grass. Even as Buller's body hit the ground, the other Volunteers were dragging their horses to a halt or trying to turn the wild, struggling animals to make good their escape.

The New Hampstead Volunteers found themselves in an unenviable position, one that steadier, better-trained troops might have been excused for spooking under. They were leaderless, almost every man's gun empty, and it took even a well-trained man time to strip foil from the combustible cartridges, ram them home into the chambers, then set on the percussion caps. It was a thing few, if any, men could do while on the back of a horse. The Volunteers were not skilled and, even without the stress of being fired at, took time to fumble their way through the difficult reloading of percussion-loaded-and-fired revolvers. Their position now left but one alternative: flight, get clear as fast as a horse could take them.

Packard, the man who might possibly have rallied them, did not know what would be best. He knew his gun was empty, and his decision was helped when a bullet hit his horse and dropped it from under him. With commendable presence of mind he kicked his feet free of the stirrups and landed on his feet in front of the onrushing rebel cavalry. A bullet tore Packard's hat from his head, and he knew what he must do. Hitting the ground, he proceeded to render a very satisfactory impersonation of a corpse. Flat on the ground, facedown and hugging himself to the grass, hearing the thunder and pound of hooves all around him, Packard lay and let his men extract themselves as best they could from the danger Buller had brought the troop into.

Demoralized and leaderless, the Volunteers dropped their

guns and scattered like quail flushed from a cornfield. Nor was their going slowed by hearing a dull, booming roar as the charge under the bridge exploded.

Dusty Fog brought his black horse to a sliding halt and looked down at the river. The Moshogen Bridge was strongly made, but it was not proof against the explosive charge. He saw the young Union lieutenant moving weakly, saw that he'd not been hurt by the flying timber. Dusty also saw that the center of the bridge was gone and the two ends sagged down into the river, the current straining against them and likely to drag them in any time. He was satisfied with the morning's work. The bridge was gone; it would be long enough before the Yankee Army could move vital supplies or heavy artillery trains over to fight against the South. They'd have the delay of traveling up or down stream to the next bridge over the river.

"Bugler, sound the recall!" Dusty called as he turned back and rode toward his men. The call rang out loud, and the Texas Light Cavalry men came back fast in answer to it. Red Blaze rode up to make his report, and Dusty acknowledged his salute. "Good work, Red. You handled your side well. I'll note it on your record."

"How about their wounded and arms?" Red inquired, indicating the unhorsed and wounded Volunteers and the discarded revolvers that lay among the dead.

It was the habit of the Confederate Army to replenish their shortage of arms with battlefield requisitions. Dusty's own troop was now armed with a consignment of new 1860 army Colt revolvers snatched from under the noses of the Yankees in the rain that had brought him his third collar bar. He looked down at the weapons on the ground and shook his head.

"Joslyns, Pettingills?" He laughed. "Not worth picking up. We'll have to leave their wounded, but it won't be long before their relief force arrives." He looked around to make sure all his men had returned. "Take a point, Kiowa. Troop, right by fours. Forward yo!"

Swinging into four-abreast formation, the troop followed Dusty away from the Moshogen Valley. Dusty had completed his assignment and wanted to lead his men clear without casualties. A shrewd commander never wasted his men's lives needlessly.

Packard lifted his head from the dirt and looked around him cautiously. He made good and sure the Confederate troop was nowhere in sight. They were fading off into the distance, traveling at a steady trot and not looking back. Now that he was safe, the big man pushed himself to his feet and surveyed the situation. Apart from two or three wounded, there was no sign of any other living Volunteers. He ignored the wounded and went to where Buller lay, facedown on the ground. One glance at the gory mess that was the back of Buller's head, told Packard that nothing could be done for his commanding officer.

Bending over, Packard took up Buller's ornate-butted, fancy-looking navy Colt. Hefting the gun, Packard sniffed. It was so like the Buller brothers to have good weapons while their men were armed with any cheap trash that could be obtained. His own revolver was a Manhattan, one of the better imitations of the Colt that were blossoming out throughout the North due to war conditions easing the vigilance of the patent office. He discarded the Manhattan, did not even trouble to go back and pick it up. The Colt would do Buller no more good, so he slid it into his own holster and bent over the still form again. Quickly Packard went through the body's pockets and took the fat wallet from inside Buller's jacket. Emptying the money from the wallet, Packard dropped it to the ground and walked toward the edge of the rim in a belated interest in the fate of the bridge they should have guarded.

Two things met Packard's gaze and attention when he looked down at the shattered timbers of the bridge. The first was a distant bunch of riders approaching the Moshogen River along the Corn Road; that would be the advance scouts of the big artillery convoy that was moving up on the battlefront and relying on crossing the bridge to reach their destination. The other thing he saw was young Cogshill lying by the side of the river. The lieutenant was trying to force himself up onto his hands and knees; he appeared to be hurt, but Packard made no attempt to go down and help him.

Packard realized that General Buller would be furious when he heard that his brother's stupidity and panic had cost the Union Army a much-needed communications link. However a scapegoat might possibly be found. As second-in-command, Cogshill's actions would come under close scrutiny. With good management most of the blame for the bridge's destruction could be laid on the lieutenant's head. General Buller would be grateful to the man who gave him the means to whitewash his brother.

Unaware of his impending danger, Lieutenant Cogshill managed to get to his feet. He swayed, and the world seemed to spin around him, for he was weak from loss of blood and from pain. He looked at the wrecked bridge and groaned to himself at the sight. This was his first independent duty and he'd failed in it. True, Major Buller was in command, but the regular officers would blame Cogshill; he was the regular officer and should show the Volunteers how to carry on in the correct manner. The blame for what would be a major setback to Grant's war plans lay heavily on Cogshill's young shoulders as he started to walk slowly up the slope, looking for what was left of the troop.

The Texas Light Cavalry were billeted on a large farm some fifty miles to the south of the Moshogen River. They'd been brought back out of the firing line for a well-earned rest and refit, so were making the most of the time. The big, comfortable old farmhouse had been taken over as quarters and mess for the officers and for the regimental office.

Behind the big main building the enlisted men made use of the outbuildings or lived in the neat, tented lines in the orchard. Beyond them, under guard, were the horse lines, the regiment's horses grazing free, remuda style under watchful men. From the left a smoking fire in the blacksmith's shop showed that the regiment's farriers and smiths were hard at work, readying the horses or arms for the next round with the Yankees. For the rest of the camp there was not much activity as the men took advantage of their leisure time and lounged around in groups talking, gambling, or cleaning their guns.

Around the camp the sentries were not relaxing. They were men born and raised in Indian country and knew that a lazy sentry often wound up as a dead sentry. So they kept to their appointed places and kept alert. That paid when the commanding officer of Troop C was around, and Captain Fog was in camp right now. He did not take kindly to sloppy, lazy sentries.

The sentry on duty at the main gates leading to the farm brought his Spenser carbine, a battlefield capture, off his arm and held it across his body as he saw a party of horsemen approaching the gates. He stood fast, watching the riders. They appeared to be three Confederate troopers, a sergeant, and a blue-coated Yankee lieutenant. The sentry guessed what this party was, an escort bringing a prisoner to the rear of the fighting area, heading him for the Southern prisoner-of-war camp at Andersonville. "Sergeant of the guard!" yelled the sentry, not moving from his place to allow the approaching party entry to the farm.

The big, lean, dark sergeant in charge of the escort lounged in his saddle, then stiffened as Dusty Fog came from the guard tent followed by Billy Jack and the sergeant of the guard. Throwing a salute, the sergeant said:

"Sergeant Ysabel, Mosby's Rangers, reporting with a prisoner, Cap'n Fog."

The man's Kentucky drawl held more than a hint of an Irish accent. Billy Jack grinned, recognizing the other as an old friend.

"Howdy, Sam," he greeted, stepping forward and holding out his hand. "Where's young Lon to? Don't see him along."

"Riding scout for Colonel John," Sam Ysabel replied, then jerked his thumb to the young Union Army lieutenant. "Just brought this Yankee officer in, Cap'n."

Dusty looked at the young prisoner and smiled in a friendly manner. "Good afternoon, mister. Dismount, please, and I'll have your horse tended. Bugler! Officer of the day!" Dusty waited until the bugle call's notes rang to a close, then looked at Ysabel. "Take your men to the cookshack and get them a meal, Sergeant. What're your orders from Colonel Mosby?"

"Deliver the prisoner to the Texas Light Cavalry, then return, either today or first thing in the morning if we got here too late."

Red Blaze came up at a run, his saber bouncing at his hip, his face a trifle flushed at the constraining clutch of his collar and cravat. Red was the officer of the day, and that meant wearing the correct uniform, discarding his comfortable skirtless tunic and wearing the one laid down in dress regulations. He came to a halt and threw Dusty a salute.

The young Union lieutenant watched all this with some interest, wondering why the men snapped into military action around this small, insignificant-looking captain. Sergeant Ysabel, the prisoner's escort, was not the sort of man who gave his respect just because of his rank, that the prisoner knew. Yet he was acting respectful and not making the word *captain* sound like a jibe as his use of other ranks often appeared to. He was sitting up and acting respectful to this young captain; so were all the others.

"Your name, mister?" Dusty inquired.

"Dailey, sir. Third Cavalry."

"Mr. Blaze, escort Mr. Dailey to your quarters and make him comfortable. Keep him with you until we can arrange to pass him back to Andersonville. I'll sign your receipt for the lieutenant, Sergeant. It'll be too late for you to head back to the Rangers today. Billy Jack, see to the accommodation."

Dusty accepted the paper that Sam Ysabel held out to him. He knew something about this dark-looking sergeant of Mosby's Rangers. Sam Ysabel was a smuggler who worked the Rio Grande, one of the best; he made his living following the night trails, running contraband. That made no difference to Dusty; his home county did not border the Rio Grande, and his father, once county sheriff, now Major Hondo Fog of the Texas Light Cavalry, never found cause to deal with smugglers. Ysabel was now a useful and respectable member of the Confederate Army and was doing an exacting job of work along with his son, the boy who was later to become one of Dusty's most loyal and trusted friends.

Red and Dailey walked off side by side. There was no antagonism in Red's attitude, for he was never the man to hold any grudge against an enemy. To Red, Dailey was just another young man, a new face and a guest to be taken care of until he could be moved on to the South. Looking back to where Dusty stood talking to Billy Jack and Sam Ysabel, Dailey asked:

"Who is that small captain?"

"Who, Dusty?" asked Red, pride in his voice. "That's Captain Fog, Troop C. I reckon you might have heard of him."

There was interest in Dailey's glance as he looked back at the small man, and admiration in his voice. "I've heard of him. He was the most talked-of officer at West Point. He isn't very old, is he?"

"Almost eighteen, couple of weeks older than me," replied Red, taking Dailey into the farmhouse, through to the rear, where he occupied a small room previously allocated to a very junior servant. He waved Dailey into the only chair and sat on the edge of the small table. "You'll be all right here, but I don't know about at Andersonville. I've heard things are a mite bad down there. I'm sorry about it, but there's nothing I can do. Was I you I wouldn't try and escape from here. It'd rile up ole Dusty, and nobody'd get no peace while he stayed riled. That'd rile the boys, and they'd get mean. You've got fifty miles across country to the nearest Yankees, and we've a sergeant called Kiowa who can track a bird through the air. Be real foolish trying to escape."

Dailey managed to smile. Escape was much on his mind at the moment; it was the only thing filling his thoughts. He was a prisoner and wanted desperately to be free, to get back to the regiment he'd so recently joined, get back into the excitement and glory of the war. At first, remembering all he'd been told about sloppy discipline and unmilitary ways of the Confederate Army, Dailey thought he would be able to escape with no great trouble. So far he'd found nothing slipshod or poorly disciplined about what rebel troops he'd seen; certainly there was none in either Mosby's Rangers or the Texas Light Cavalry, both of whom were armed, trained, and equipped as well as any regular Union regiment. He'd been given no chance to escape on the journey to this farm and doubted if he would get a chance while here. What he'd seen so far warned him of that.

There was a knock at the door, and Dusty came in. Dailey came to his feet and slammed into a rigid brace, for he knew that here was an officer who would expect the correct military courtesies extended. Red also came to his feet, a sheepish grin on his face.

"At ease, gentlemen," said Dusty, then grinned at his cousin. "Everything all right?"

"Sure, Dusty. We'll get by."

Dusty sat on the edge of Red's bed and smiled at Dailey. It

was a relaxed, friendly smile as he waved them to their seats again.

"Relax, Mr. Dailey, we're not after tricking any military secrets out of you. If you don't mind me asking, how did you come to get captured?"

"On a routine patrol," replied Dailey, cheeks flushing at the thought. "I was taking a small detail out in safe territory, or should have been according to our reports. Our information was that there were no enemy troops in the area, and we must have been taking things easy. I've never seen anything like it in my life, the way the Mosby men just seemed to come out of the ground. We were in open country, and they just seemed to come from nowhere. They took us with hardly a shot fired, disarmed and set my men afoot, then took me with them."

"The fortunes of war, mister," drawled Dusty, reading the misery in the young man's voice. He'd lost his patrol and been captured on what was probably his first independent command. "One of the first rules when fighting light cavalry is expect anything, regard any formation with suspicion, and be ready for them where they shouldn't be."

In years to come, when serving as an Indian fighting officer, Dailey was to remember that advice, save the lives of his men, and prevent his scalp from decorating a Sioux lodge. Right now he was too miserable at being taken prisoner to worry about good or bad advice. He wanted to talk and take his mind off his misery.

"You're the same Captain Fog who blew up the Moshogen Bridge, aren't you?"

"The same."

"It made a real tangle of our communications, I'll tell you. We'd a big convoy moving to the front, and they were delayed badly by having to backtrack and find another crossing. The court-martial convenes on Monday morning."

Dusty was surprised at Dailey's bitterness as he mentioned the court-martial, and wondered at it. The young lieutenant must have expected the major commanding the ineffective guard detail to be court-martialed for his failure to prevent the destruction of the bridge. Then Dusty remembered Red's report.

"I thought you said you killed that major in command of the Yankees, Red."

"I thought so, too. I allowed to have hit him twice, second time in the head. Way he went down, I figured he was dead."

"He is," Dailey put in.

"Who're they court-martialing, then?" asked Dusty.

"Kirby Cogshill."

"Who's he?"

"The lieutenant who rode second-in-command of the guard detail."

"The lieutenant," snapped Dusty, face creasing in a frown. "How do you mean, court-martialing him. What were the charges?"

"Dereliction of his duty, cowardice in the face of the enemy, deserting his command, and failing to obey a lawful given order by a superior officer," answered Dailey bitterly. "Any one of them carrying the death penalty under the circumstances. They say he ran away from the fight at the top of the slope, left his men."

Dusty and Red exchanged looks, hardly believing their ears. It was Dusty who spoke, his voice hard and angry.

"That's a damned lie. The lieutenant was just about the only one who made any attempt at the correct performance of his duties. He'd wanted to make a search of the woods where we were hidden, and the major wouldn't. He tried to stop the men going after Red on the other side, must have guessed what was happening. Then he came back to try and stop two of us blowing the bridge up."

Dailey stared at Dusty, a faint glimmer of hope in his eyes. "I know Kirby Cogshill. He was honor cadet of our year and we were roommates at the Point. I knew he wouldn't do any of the things they were saying about him. It's that damned Packard, the sergeant-major—he's promoted to first lieutenant for his part in the fight or something—and I can guess what the something is. These damned volunteer regiments are all the same, they's not worth the . . ."

The words died off as Dailey realized that the Texas Light

Cavalry was, to all intents and purposes, a volunteer regiment too. Dusty ignored the regular soldier's contempt for volunteers, for he was thinking about the injustice being done to a good and brave young officer.

"Where's this court-martial to be held?" he asked.

"In the Moshogen town courthouse on Monday."

"Monday, huh?"

"Yes, sir," agreed Dailey, forgetting these two men were his enemies and that he was a prisoner. Here were two men who knew nearly everything that happened on the banks of the Moshogen River. They might be able to help his friend, prove that Kirby Cogshill was not guilty of the charges leveled against him. "If you ask me," he went on hotly, "this is all part of a plan to whitewash General Buller's brother. It wouldn't do Bully Buller's political aspirations any good to have it known his brother was a stupid, incompetent fool, one who caused the North to lose a valuable bridge when it was needed. That's why old Kirby's being thrown to the wolves."

"That could be, mister," Dusty agreed, coming to his feet and walking to the door. "Excuse me, please."

Dailey watched the door close behind Dusty and returned to Red with a puzzled frown. He'd been hoping to talk with Dusty to try to work out some way word could be sent to the Union Army, helping to clear his friend.

"What's wrong?" he asked. "Did I say something out of line?"

"Something's worrying Dusty," Red replied thoughtfully. He knew his cousin very well and could almost have said what Dusty was going to do. Red hoped his guess would prove wrong and Dusty would not be doing what Red suspected he was.

Dusty went down the stairs and to the front of the house. In an alcove next to the library door a white-haired master-sergeant was working on some papers. He looked up as Dusty came to the desk.

"I'd like to see the general, Tom." Dusty requested.

"He's with Sheldon and Stuart, told me not to disturb him unless it was real important."

"It's important."

The master-sergeant came to his feet and went into the library, closing the door behind him. A few moments later he came out again and held the door open. "Go right in, Cap'n," he said.

Dusty entered the room, crossed to the big table at one side, and halted in a rigid brace, hand going up in a smart salute. The three men seated at the table watched him; there was a look of tolerant pleasure in the way they eyed the small young man. Ole Devil Hardin sat in the center of the group, a tall, spare, tanned man with hard black eyes. His sharp, drawn, grim fighting-man's face relaxed in a rare smile as he looked at his favorite nephew. To Hardin's right, stocky, black-bearded, and hard-looking, was General Bushrod Sheldon. To the left, lean, spare, younger, and handsome, with a cavalry man's look about him even while he sat on a chair, was General J. E. B. Stuart. Dusty felt a touch of pride in the way these three men showed approval when they looked at him.

Dropping his eyes to Dusty's skirtless tunic, General Sheldon gave a snort. "I see you've gone for Mark Counter's dress style."

Dusty allowed a smile to flicker on his face. He did not, as yet, know Mark Counter, except by repute. Mark Counter was a lieutenant in Sheldon's regiment, the son of a rich Big Bend rancher. Being something of a dandy dresser, Mark brought his own style of uniform into the Cavalry, the skirtless tunic being one of his innovations. It was a style of uniform Dusty, for all his strict ways, adopted as being a useful idea.

"With the general's permission, I claim it's the best dress for a mounted, fighting soldier," answered Dusty politely.

Jeb Stuart chuckled and Sheldon snorted like a walrus. The new style of uniform was a cause of much controversy among the Confederate Army brass, although little was done officially to either approve or condemn it.

Ole Devil Hardin watched Dusty, knowing something important was bothering the youngster, and waited to hear why Dusty came in to interrupt an important conference.

Before he could speak, Ole Devil was given another interruption. The door at the other end of the room opened and a small, smiling Oriental man entered, carrying a tray with glasses and a bottle of bourbon. The man, Ole Devil's personal servant, was Tommy Okasi, thought to be Chinese, but actually Japanese, come to the United States by clipper ship to avoid some trouble in his own land. Ole Devil had found him in New Orleans and had taken him on, gaining a loyal friend and a faithful servant. Tommy had settled in the Rio Hondo country of Texas, and of all the numerous Hardin, Blaze, and Fog children Dusty was his favorite boy. To Dusty, smallest of them all, Tommy Okasi had taught certain fighting tricks, which more than offset his lack of inches and gave him a terrific advantage over much bigger and stronger men.

"What can we do for you, Dustine?" Ole Devil asked.

Dusty explained and had the pleasure of seeing three men, who were noted among the hard-gambling Southern gentlemen as poker players, show a lot more surprise than was usual. At the end of his request Ole Devil barked:

"That's out of the question. You can't put yourself into the Yankee Army's hands. Certainly not!"

"Devil's right!" Sheldon growled. "Let 'em shoot that fool shavetail, save us the trouble of doing it."

"He's innocent, sir," objected Dusty. "A promising young officer's name and honor's being dragged in the mud to help clear the name of a stupid, incompetent fool—"

"Not the first time it's happened, and likely won't be the last," answered Sheldon. "Let him take his chance."

Jeb Stuart smiled, watched the faces of the other men. He was the youngest of the trio of generals and could guess what was making Dusty act in such a manner. So could Sheldon and Hardin, but they were older and looked on life a bit more seriously. Stuart did not say anything, just sat back and watched the others, reserving his opinion until later.

"It's without precedent!" Sheldon snapped. "An officer going to give evidence at the court-martial of an enemy."

"It is, sir," agreed Dusty, "but every precedent was without precedent the first time it was done and formed the precedent."

The three generals sat back and exchanged glances. The chivalry of war was not yet debased and dead, and a Southern gentleman was that, a gentleman, with everything the words implied. They were bound by a code of honor as hard and firm as any other chivalrous code in the world. They all knew what a court-martial on such charges would mean to a career officer. Even if the death penalty was not given, it would break young Cogshill and ruin him. Yet, for all of that, it would be a risky thing to allow a valuable man like Dusty to go into the Union Army hands. There were men in the Union Army, the new set of officers, who would not object to this chance of taking one of the South's three top raiders prisoner, even if he had come to give evidence at a court-martial.

"I suppose you've made up your mind to go through with it, Captain?" Sheldon asked. "Even without permission."

"If necessary, sir. Even without permission."

Once more there was that exchange of glances and half-hidden smiles. They all knew Dusty meant every word he said. He would go to the Moshogen courthouse to give evidence before the court-martial and chance his luck and skill to escape after doing so. The only way to prevent him would be to slap him under guard, and they knew his troop would not stand for that. They might just as well give in and let him go, helping him all they could.

"I suppose you know how you'll do it?" Hardin made a statement of the words rather than a question. He knew Dusty was not blindly charging into something without knowing how it could be handled with the fewest risks.

"Yes, sir. We can send the prisoner, Mr. Dailey, back with a message. I think he'll give us his word not to fight against the Confederacy until an exchange has been made. He can deliver my message to the court and make arrangements for a reply to be brought."

"Damn it to hell!" Sheldon bellowed, annoyed at the casual way Dusty was taking all this. "You can't trust Yankees, they can't even trust each other. Look at how they treated Bosanquet over that Quaker wagon massacre."

Dusty did not reply to this, although he knew the story. A Union Army officer, Major Kliddoe, wiped out a small wagon train of Quakers, then laid the blame on his commanding officer, Colonel Bosanquet, who was broken for it. Dusty knew Kliddoe to be the same kind of man as the South's William Clarke Quantrel, a murdering plunderer who used his side's flag as an excuse for looting and outrage. They were neither of them typical of the other men who fought for both sides.

"I think we could trust Grant, Sherman, or Sheridan and take their word on this matter, sir," Dusty drawled. "They're regular officers and would want to help clear another regular's name."

Sheldon was also a regular officer and knew the close bonds that linked one professional soldier to the others. When one found himself in trouble, the others would do everything possible to help him out of it.

"There's that to it," he grudgingly conceded. "Cogshill? Would that be Will Cogshill's boy, Kirby?"

"That was the name Mr. Dailey gave me, sir."

"Will and I served together in the Mexican War. Good soldier. I was his best man," Sheldon said grimly. "Young Kirby was a good boy at the Point, made Best Cadet of his year, I heard. Hear Will's commanding the Third Cavalry over to Moshogen—" He stopped as a thought hit him. "Hell fire, that means Will's going to have to lay on the court-martial for young Kirby—for his own son on those charges."

"It looks bad," Stuart spoke up. "We'll help you, Dusty."

"Thank you, sir. I never doubted it."

"It doesn't mean we don't think you're a damned hot-headed young fool for doing it," barked Sheldon.

"Know something, sir?" Dusty answered with a frank, open smile. "So do I."

"Will Mosby object to you releasing his prisoner?" Hardin inquired.

"I doubt it, sir. Not when he knows the full circumstances.

He'd do the same thing himself," answered Dusty. "Besides . . ."

"Yes?"

"I can always catch him a young Yankee shavetail in exchange—after I get back from Moshogen."

Dusty returned to Red's room and found it empty, so he made his way to the mess hall and found his cousin, along with the other junior officers of the regiment, entertaining Dailey. The young men who led the troops of the Texas Light Cavalry greeted Dusty rowdily, for a boisterous party was in full swing. Dusty waved aside offers of a drink and went to Dailey.

"I'd like to see you in my room, Mr. Dailey."

"Certainly, sir," Dailey replied and apologized to the others for leaving the party. He and Red followed Dusty from the room and through to the rear, where the officers were quartered. Dusty's room was not much larger or better furnished than Red's quarters, and Dusty waved Dailey into a chair. Dusty sat at the table and took up a pen, pulled a sheet of paper toward him, while the other two waited for him to say why he had brought them from a party.

"I understand you're a good friend of Mr. Cogshill?"

"A very good friend, sir. We were roommates at West Point and hoped to serve together in his father's regiment, but Kirby was placed in the Volunteers."

"You'd be pleased to help him, then?"

"Of course," Dailey replied. It went without saying he would be willing to do anything he could to help a friend in time of need. He could not see how he was in any position to help Kirby Cogshill, not as a prisoner headed for Andersonville.

Dailey watched Dusty's face, not able to guess what the questions were leading up to. He could hardly understand Dusty's interest in Cogshill's welfare and had no inkling of what Dusty was thinking. The small Texan was not the sort to torment a prisoner with false hopes, that Dailey was sure of. There was more to the questions than first met the eye. The young officer almost guessed what lay behind the questions, but he shrugged off the idea as too fantastic for words. No man would go to such lengths to help an enemy.

That was where Dailey made his mistake. There was one man who not only would go to such lengths but was already making plans to do it.

"I'll give you a chance to help Mr. Cogshill," Dusty went on, watching the other's face all the time. "I'll have a letter for you to deliver to the president of the court-martial. In return you'll be expected to sign a cartel and give your assurance that you won't fight against the Army of the Confederacy until such time as an exchange of prisoners is arranged and carried out. Do I have your word?"

Dailey stared at Dusty without speaking for a long moment. He could not think straight; his mind appeared to have become clogged and jumbled. There was only one reply he could give to the generous offer.

"You have my word, sir. I'll sign anything."

Dusty Fog was no fool. He knew the risks he was running and was not unduly worried by them. The thought that this might be a plot arranged by some overbright Union Army man also occurred to him, although he doubted it. He'd watched Dailey's face carefully, trying to see some expression that would warn him. There'd been no sign, no flickering, furtive, hint of triumph that might serve as warning to Dusty, nothing but interest. It was too much to believe this might be a clever plan to trap Dusty, there was too much against it. The young lieutenant could not have known he would be captured or the Union Army would have made sure he didn't also let the Confederates get good arms and horses. Even had it all been a plot, they could not have known Dailey would be delivered to the Texas Light Cavalry. Mosby usually handed his prisoners over to the nearest formal Confederate regiment, but there was no way the Yankees could know Dailey would be brought to the Texas Light Cavalry.

With this in mind Dusty started to write.

"Come and see General Hardin, Mr. Dailey," he suggested as he finished his letter to the president of the court-martial. "All being well, we should be able to send you back to the

Union Army at dawn tomorrow. I'll want you to go as escort for Mr. Dailey, Red. Take Kiowa and six men with you. Warn them off for it, ready. Mr. Dailey, you'll be traveling under flag of truce. You can go back to the mess now. I'll send for you when we've done, Red."

Red Blaze did not argue. He followed a rule of never going nearer to his Uncle Devil than was necessary; that way he hoped to avoid attracting any unpleasant military attentions.

Dusty and Dailey went toward the library, and now there was no thought of escape in the prisoner's mind. Two men were working on some papers at the desk, the master-sergeant and Dusty's father. Hondo Fog straightened up, a tall, wide-shouldered man wearing a major's uniform and with a pipe clenched between his teeth. He looked his eldest son over with a grin playing on his lips. Removing the pipe, he pointed the stem at Dusty.

"You always could stir up a hornet's nest, boy. This time you've done better than ever. I've never seen Bushrod Sheldon so riled."

"Sounds likely, sir," Dusty replied, grinning broadly. "He's torn between his mistrust of the Yankees and a desire to help out an old friend." Then Dusty forgot Sheldon and got down to business. "I'll want certified true copies of such parts of Red and my reports as cover Lieutenant Cogshill's behavior at the bridge."

"Tom's doing that right now," Hondo replied. "Here's a copy of the letter, Mr. Dailey—isn't it?—will be taking with him."

Dusty accepted the letter and read it through. It was written in the stilted, formal language of military circles and asked for free, unrestricted passage of escort of himself, Billy Jack, and one servant, for the purpose of giving evidence at the forthcoming court-martial. It also asked for guarantee to be given that Dusty would be allowed to return freely to the Confederate lines after concluding his business. Dusty could see the hand of Bushrod Sheldon involved in this; the general would want something really certain before he allowed Dusty to go. The letter was satisfactory, and

Dusty was sure it would get fast results. He passed it back to his father and asked if he could see General Hardin.

"He'll be ready for you in a few minutes, Dusty," Hondo replied.

"I've told Red to be ready to escort Mr. Dailey in the morning. For all of that, he'll have some fast moving to do. The court convenes on Monday, and today's Wednesday. It doesn't give much time at all."

Dusty was sure there would be some fast moving done when his letter reached official Union hands. The regular-army men would be only too willing to help one of their kind clear his name, and Dusty's letter gave a hope of doing just that. So his letter would be moved through the usually slow channels at a good speed. Colonel Cogshill was one who would see to that and there were others higher up who would be just as eager to unblock slow-moving channels. The letter would most probably be sent by fast-riding courier to the commanding general and acted upon.

Proof of Dusty's guesswork came on Saturday, when a courier came from the fighting line, having been sent back with the letter that was brought under flag of truce from the Union side that morning. Dusty came on the run from where he'd been taking his troop at saber practice.

In Hardin's office Dusty found the general and his father waiting for him. Hardin held out a letter. "Here, boy. This just come in. They're granting you and your party unrestricted passage. You're to meet Major Hamley, Third Cavalry, at Quail Ridge, and he'll be your escort."

"There's more than just that to it, isn't there, sir?" asked Dusty, for he could read as much in Ole Devil's tones.

"Not much. Just that the letter was signed jointly by Grant, Sherman, Phil Sheridan—and Abe Lincoln."

Dusty took the letter, his face showing some of the surprise he felt. Here was patronage on a grand scale. He'd expected Sherman, as commanding general, to take an interest, possibly Sheridan and Grant as regular soldiers, to show some interest in the matter. But Lincoln was the president of the United States, and no soldier. It was hard to understand his motive, unless he was as fair-minded, honest, and justice-loving as the Yankees tried to claim he was.

Whatever the reason, the proof was in Dusty's hand, in the letter signed by the top four men of the Union. Another paragraph caught Dusty's eye, a further guarantee of his safety.

"Colonel Sir Charles Houghton-Rand and Colonel Baron Ulrich von Dettmer, military observers of Great Britain and Germany, will be on hand all the time, having both read and received copies of this letter."

"Which same means I'll likely be sent back on the hoof," remarked Dusty.

There could be no plot to capture Dusty about this business now, no treacherous moves afoot. Not when such a letter was signed by the president himself and with two foreign military observers on hand.

"Looks that way," agreed Ole Devil. "You still aim to go through with it?"

"I couldn't do otherwise now, sir," replied Dusty. "I'll warn Billy Jack to be ready to pull out at one o'clock. We'll move up to Quail Ridge and spend the night with the forward troops, then cross over tomorrow morning. Should be back here by Wednesday at the latest."

"I hope you are, boy. Watch Buller all the same. He's not going to take kindly to your arriving and spoiling his plans."

"That's right, boy," agreed Hondo Fog. "He'll likely try to do something about it. Watch him."

"I'll do just that," promised Dusty and turned to leave.

At one o'clock Dusty swung afork his big black horse and watched Billy Jack approaching with the old soldier who was Dusty's striker. The men were riding their horses, and the soldier, Unwin, led a pony with Dusty's box aboard.

Red Blaze came to his cousin's side, worry plain on his face. "If you're not back by Wednesday, I'll bring the troop and get you out."

"You won't!" Dusty snapped, knowing Red was quite likely to try to do just what he said. "That's an order, Mr. Blaze. Do I have to give it you in writing?"

Stiffening to a brace, Red replied. "No, sir." He felt no

annoyance at Dusty's words, only worry that his cousin should be risking going into the hands of the Union Army. "It's just that I—"

"You're worse than an old hen, Red," replied Dusty, holding out his hand. "Don't you worry none, they'll play fair with me."

"I sure wish I'd your confidence," Red growled. "What do you want me to do while you're gone?"

"Keep up the troop training that I've laid down in my orders. And don't cut out any of the drill training. It won't do the troop any harm—or you."

Red managed a weak grin at this jibe on his dislike and avoidance of drill and parade-ground soldiering. He watched Dusty riding through the farm gates with a feeling of foreboding and a strong lacing of pride. There were not many men who would take such a risk to help an enemy. Along with Turner Ashby and John Singleton Mosby, Dusty was high on the Union Army's list of most-wanted Southern officers. His unorthodox tactics made him one of the men the Union Army talked about, and some of them might look on it as a god-sent opportunity, having him dropped into their hands that way. Red was full of misgivings as he turned to make for the mess. One thing he knew for sure. If Dusty did not come back by Thursday at the latest, Red aimed to take the troop, orders to the contrary or not, and make a try at prying Dusty free.

There were no snags met by Dusty on his way to Quail Ridge. It was, for the most part, open country and in Southern hands. The Union Army might have many advantages over the South in arms and equipment, but they never saw the day when their cavalry could equal the South's for sheer raiding daring. So Dusty found no trouble in reaching the forward area and stayed the night as arranged with a Confederate Infantry regiment. He did not know any of the officers, although he was known to all of them. What surprised him was that his mission was known, a thing he was not too happy about, even though he knew such an unusual incident would be talked about from one end of the army to the other. The colonel of the infantry regiment clearly thought Dusty should not be taking such a risk, but did not say so.

The following morning the camp was disturbed by a bugle blowing. Men turned out and took up their defensive positions as a Union Army major rode toward them, followed by a bugler blowing loud calls and a soldier carrying a large white flag. This was the accepted way of requesting a truce, bugle blowing to show no surprise was intended and white flag to advertise the pacific intentions of the party.

Dusty felt just a little uneasy as he shook hands with his host, then mounted and rode out, followed by Billy Jack and Unwin, to meet the Union Army party. The two groups came to a halt about fifty yards from the Confederate lines. Dusty, being the junior officer, saluted first.

"Captain Fog, Troop C. Texas Light Cavalry, with party as arranged, sir."

"Major Hamley, Third Cavalry," replied the Union officer, saluting in return to Dusty's compliment. He appeared to doubt his eyes, wondering if this small young man could possibly be the famous Dusty Fog. "If you'll accompany me, Captain."

Dusty rode forward with Hamley, his two men following behind him. Unwin did not appear bothered, but he was a long-serving old-timer and used to taking whatever fate offered him. Billy Jack was for once feeling as worried as he always looked. He did not know of the letter, of the guarantees made for their safe return, and it said much for his faith in Dusty that Billy Jack was going along with his captain into the hands of the enemy.

They rode side by side across the open land that separated the two warring armies, the big Union major and the small Confederate captain. The blue-clad Union troops looked on without emotion as the party passed through their lines. The enlisted men gave no sign of hostility toward their enemies, and such officers as they passed showed a half-hidden approval, giving Dusty their unspoken blessing in what was to come. In the short time he'd been associated with the Union Army, General Buller had established something of a reputation as a bully, an uncouth brute, and made few if any friends. So Dusty was given the unspoken support of many of the Union men, in that he was going against General Buller.

The party rode on, following a straighter route than the one used by Dusty on his return from the raid that destroyed the Moshogen Bridge. This time they used the Corn Road and made good time along it. At the Moshogen River Dusty found that the bridge was not rebuilt, although the Union Army was working hard on it. A small ferry was being used to transport horsemen or foot soldiers across, but there was no way that large quantities of heavy traffic could cross at this point. There was a company of infantry camped on either side of the river now and a troop of cavalry near at hand, a strong guard for one place.

Hamley saw where Dusty was looking and laughed. "That's a famous example of the art of locking the door after the horse is stolen. Don't worry, Captain, you won't be catching us out like that again. When the bridge's rebuilt, there'll be a strong guard permanently on it. Regular soldiers, too."

Dusty grinned, looking younger and more boyish than ever. "Looks like there is right now."

It was something of a tribute to himself and his troop that their effort was treated in such a manner. There was more than just the destruction of the bridge to be counted here. That in itself was a shrewd, hard, and damaging blow, but there was more. Two companies of infantry and a troop of cavalry were tied down on a boring guard duty, held away from the battlefield. More than ever, Dusty could see the value of his kind of tactics against an enemy army. Light Cavalry, striking overland, traveling fast, and hitting where they were least expected could make hard and damaging blows out of all proportion to the size of the command.

Crossing the Moshogen River on the ferry, the party resumed its journey along the Corn Road. Hamley watched Dusty and wondered how one so young could handle himself with such perfect self-control. They talked as they rode, idle talk of small and unimportant things. Hamley made no attempts to pump Dusty for information, and in return

Dusty studiously avoided using his time to study the Union Army's setup on the northern side of the river. He ignored the various military details they passed, for he was a Southern gentleman and on his honor here. He would not abuse the privilege given to him, and it said much for the code of the Southern men that Hamley accepted Dusty's word and did not insist on either steering him along a route where he could see nothing, nor on blindfolding him and his party.

Behind Dusty, Billy Jack and Unwin rode easily, talking with the two Union soldiers, their talk less formal and more boisterous. Neither of the men thought to look around them, and Billy Jack was a scout of note. He'd got his orders from Dusty, and a man didn't disobey Captain Fog's orders. Not twice, anyway.

Moshogen Town lay in a fold of land about a mile from the bridge. It was a small, sedate, sleepy town where, before the war, little if anything ever happened to change the even temper of the people. War, and their proximity to the Moshogen Bridge, brought life, bustle, and some prosperity to the small town, even though it had twice changed hands bloodlessly. The Union Army now held it, the Third Cavalry being in residence at the moment; however, there was always the chance the Confederate forces might return, drive out the Yankees, and take control once more.

A Confederate Army officer and two men, riding fully armed and with a small Union Army party, caused some slight stir as they went along Moshogen's main street to the big house taken over by the Third Cavalry for officers' quarters. The citizens were interested, but only slightly, and there were no demonstrations for or against Dusty's party. The town lay on the Mason-Dixon Line, and the citizens had learned early not to show any great sympathy for either side of the conflict. A man could never say for sure which side would be in command of the town next. The fortunes of war might see the Stars and Stripes of the Union hauled down and the Stars and Bars of the Confederacy flying in their place. So the citizens of the town, those who remained, not joining one or the other army, adopted a passive attitude and gave their support to whichever side was in control at the moment.

Hamley led Dusty and his men around to the rear of the big old house the Third Cavalry used as their headquarters. The house was one of the big, old colonial-style buildings, much like the one the Texas Light Cavalry were using to the south. The horse lines of the regiment were in the big orchard behind the building, and Hamley led the party to them.

"If you'll tell your men to leave their mounts here, Captain," he said as he dismounted. "I've arranged for your horse to have a stall in the stables."

Dusty nodded in agreement, his attention taken by a big, burly man who was standing watching them. The man wore the uniform of a lieutenant of the Union Army, his face was hard and brutal, and there was a calculating glint in his eyes as he watched them dismount. Then he started forward, his hand loosening the top of his holster as he walked toward Dusty.

"You're the lousy reb who killed Major Buller, aren't you?"

Hamley swung around, annoyance plain on his face as he looked at the big man. His voice was hard as he barked, "That's enough from you, Mr. Packard."

Packard looked as if he had been drinking. There was a mean, slit-eyed look about his eyes and a lurching in his step, which gave more than casual proof to the assumption. He looked at Dusty, never even glancing at Hamley.

"Yeah?" he snarled. "I ain't forgetting he killed the major."

Dusty frowned. If Packard had been one of his lieutenants, Dusty would have acted with some speed and taught him a lesson he'd never forget. Dusty was a strict disciplinarian and would never stand for an officer under him being drunk and acting like this one, in front of enlisted men.

Then Dusty's eyes narrowed and he tensed slightly. The man might look as if he was drunk, but some instinct warned Dusty he was not. The man was acting drunk. He might have had a couple of whiskies to make his breath smell, but that was all. He was sober and knew what he was doing. Dusty could rely on his judgment and instinct in a manner of this nature. He could also rely on his memory. The name Packard meant something to him. It was the name of Buller's sergeant-major, the one who was promoted for his part in the battle at the Moshogen Bridge.

"You've got things all wrong, mister," replied Dusty, holding his voice even and watching the other man. "I didn't kill any of your men. I wounded Mr. Cogshill, but any of the killing was done by my troop. It was all over before I reached the top of the slope."

"Is that right?" sneered Packard, moving closer, still looking as if he were carrying a full load of brave-maker.

Then his fist shot out, straight at Dusty's head. It was a beautiful punch, thrown with all Packard's weight and power behind it, driven by a heavy body and a mighty muscled arm throwing the knotted fist. It was the sort of blow Packard used to fell any worker who complained at the long hours or working conditions in Buller's factory, the sort of blow that ended a fight before it got started. Straight for Dusty's head the fist flew; it was sent hard enough to knock him unconscious for a long time—had it landed.

Dusty moved faster than Hamley or Packard ever saw a man move. He sidestepped, catching Packard's wrist and heaving. The result was highly spectacular. Packard was off-balance, his weight thrown forward and expecting to smash the fist into Dusty's face. Instead he went flying forward, hurled by his own body weight and the pull. The big man was no mean hand in a fight, but he was given no chance to show his talent. He struck at what he thought was an unprepared man and found he'd a tiger by the tail. He staggered forward and lost his balance, crashed down hard, and rolled to his knees. His hand went to the holster and almost reached the ornate butt of the navy Colt.

"Hold it right there!"

Dusty's flat barked warning came as his left hand flipped across his body to bring the bone-handled Colt from his right holster; the hammer was drawn back under his thumb, and his finger held back the trigger. It was all done in a flickering half second, faster than Packard could even think.

Hamley's angry yelled warning died off half done, but

Packard was not even interested; his eyes were on the gun that was lined on him. Like most people who first saw a frontier-trained gun-fighting man in action, he could hardly believe his eyes. He'd no conception of just how fast or deadly such a man could be. Even now he was not sure where the gun had come from, how it came to be in Dusty's hand. All Packard knew was he'd got to stop playing with guns against such a man.

"On your feet, Packard!" Hamley barked, face working angrily at the other man's actions. "Confine yourself to your quarters, mister. I'm sending you back to your regiment under arrest."

Packard's hand left the gun holster and he slapped the flap closed. He knew that in any matter concerning the use of guns he was beaten by this small Texan. It would have to be handled some other way, this plan of his. Slowly he got to his feet and stood mouthing curses, making no move to go to his quarters. Hamley's face grew even redder at the refusal to obey orders.

Holstering his gun, Dusty turned away. It was not polite for a visiting officer from another army to watch an internal trouble between two officers of the army he was visiting, even if the trouble did directly concern him. So Dusty turned to give Billy Jack orders about his conduct during the stay with the Yankee Army. He heard Hamley's angry shout, the sound of hard feet behind him, then two huge arms locked around him from behind. The arms tightened around his waist, under his own arms, crushing at him with savage and brutal strength. Dusty grunted in pain as Packard put on pressure in an attempt to crush the breath from him and break his ribs. The big man's face showed his triumph as he put on more pressure, bunching his powerful muscles for the effort and ignoring Hamley's angry shouts to let go. Billy Jack caught the major's hand as he began to draw his gun. There was a grin on Billy Jack's miserable face as he watched the way Dusty's feet were moving.

"Hold hard there, Major," he drawled mournfully. "That big *hombre*'s going to get him one real fast, free, and friendly lesson of how the Texas Light handles a drunk,"—

he paused, and the grin grew even broader—"even if the same drunk ain't so drunk as he acts." Which proved that Billy Jack might talk slow, look to have all the cares in the world, but was still a real quick-thinking man whose perceptions were just as quick and all-seeing as his commanding officer's.

Hamley frowned, holding his gun yet not drawing it. Before he could decide what he should do about it, he was too late.

Dusty moved his feet until they were between Hamley's widespread legs and slightly behind Packard's big feet. The small Texan was grunting in pain but he was still able to think and act even though the breath was being crushed from his body. He made no attempt to break the crushing pressure, knowing that his strength was as nothing compared with the other man's. Dropping his hands, he got them around the outside and back of Packard's thighs. Then Dusty bent slightly and lifted. It looked almost as if he was giving the huge man a piggyback ride. Once more Dusty's strength took Packard by surprise, and before the big man could make up his mind how to handle this unusual situation, he felt Dusty bending forward. Packard's own weight worked as a pivot, his hands lost their hold, and he felt himself falling to the ground. There was no time for him to protect his head as he fell, and it crashed onto the ground with a sickening thud. Packard's big frame crumpled as if it were boned and he lay without moving.

"Sure hope he's all right," remarked Billy Jack unhappily, although he hoped no such thing.

So did Dusty, although he was a little more sincere in his hope. The jujitsu throw, called *seoi-age,* the lifting shoulder throw, taught him by Ole Devil's servant, was very effective. It was also deadly dangerous in use, and in training or practice was termed complete just by lifting the other man from his feet. To do the throw in earnest as Dusty did with Packard, was likely to wind up with the receiver breaking his neck, or at least with a fractured skull. Bending down, Dusty looked at the still form on the ground and felt something like relief to see the neck was not broken. If there were other injuries, Dusty could not see, but he expected there would be. Packard had lit down hard, headfirst, and there was probably some serious damage.

Hamley, face red with anger and mortification, but shaken by the apparent ease with which Dusty handled a much larger man, moved forward. He turned and bellowed his anger at the enlisted men who gathered from where they'd been policing the horse lines. The men had gathered around and stood chattering excitedly, pointing out to each other what happened.

"Four of you carry Packard to the guardhouse and leave him there," Hamley growled. "You, Sergeant, my compliments to the post surgeon; tell him to attend to Mr. Packard and report to me on his condition."

Hamley felt suddenly worried; the full awareness of what had just occurred came to him. His face reddened with both anger and embarrassment at Packard's action. His regiment's honor, more, the honor of the United States of America was at stake. He knew full well the backing behind bringing Captain Fog to Moshogen, knew of the letter and who had signed it. Dusty Fog was in Moshogen under a guarantee of safety, and he might have been seriously injured or killed. Packard's actions might be taken as the behavior of a drunk, but he was wearing the uniform of a lieutenant of the Union Army, and such an action could hardly be passed over. Then Hamley remembered the two military observers who'd come to make sure the terms of the letter were carried out. He did not know how Houghton-Rand or von Dettmer would take the news that Dusty had been attacked by a drunkard the moment he arrived.

"I'd like to apologize for Packard's actions, Captain Fog," he said sincerely. "Damn him for a drunken trouble-maker. I'll have him court-martialed and dismissed for this."

"You don't need to apologize, sir," replied Dusty. "He wasn't of your regiment, and I attach no blame to you."

Hamley did not try to hide his relief at the words. He knew full well how much importance Sherman attached to this visit, and it would go badly for Hamley if anything should happen to Dusty. He could see that Dusty did not appear to be unduly worried by the attempted attack and put it down to Dusty laying it all on the temper of an ill-bred, drunken lout.

In this surmise Hamley was far from right. Dusty did not blame the major of the Third Cavalry for the attack. He did not put it down to the action of a drunk either. Dusty *knew* Packard was far from drunk. The man had been cold sober and probably under orders from General Buller to either kill or injure the small Texan, preventing him giving his evidence at the court-martial.

There was a grin on Dusty's face, a grin that both Billy Jack and Unwin knew all too well, even if Hamley did not. It was the grim-lipped grin that only came when danger was thickest and it always heralded trouble for someone. Dusty knew his life was in danger every minute he was here in Moshogen, that he was dealing with a powerful man who was rich enough to hire men like Packard. General Buller was a hard and ruthless man, not one to be worried by small matters like his country's honor. He would try everything in his power to remove this small Texan who came to prevent an innocent man from being sacrificed for the Buller pride. Buller was not going to stand back and watch Dusty spoil the plan to whitewash his brother's name, and Buller must guess that Dusty alone could possibly clear young Cogshill of the charges falsely laid against him.

"Where at's General Buller now, Major?" Dusty asked innocently, watching the soldiers carrying Packard away. "That was one of his men, wasn't it?"

"It was, Packard, the sergeant-major who was with Charlie Buller at the Moshogen Bridge. General Buller promoted him for his part in the action. Buller's not in Moshogen. General Grant ordered both Colonel Cogshill and Buller to join him until after the court-martial."

"Grant? Is he near to hand?"

"Very near," answered Hamley, and something in his voice told Dusty there was more than just the bald statement implied. "Very well guarded, too."

Dusty smiled at his compliment to the way he and his two raiding colleagues, Mosby and Ashby, were acting. No

Union Army staff officer could feel safe anywhere within striking distance of the Confederate lines, not when a fast-riding cavalry troop might suddenly appear, swoop down, and snatch him from safety to be dumped in the Andersonville prisoner-of-war camp. He could see that General U. S. Grant, commander-in-chief of the Union Army, was concerned that the trial should go off without a hitch. General Buller and Colonel Cogshill both being taken away from the town showed that.

For all his absence, Buller was not going to sit back mildly and allow Dusty to ruin his plan to exculpate his brother. Dusty knew that; he also knew that he must be ready to meet other attempts on his life and they might be shrewder, more subtle than this one.

They saw to the horses, leaving Billy Jack and Unwin's mounts in the horse lines of Hamley's company, tactfully overlooking the U.S. brand the horses carried. It was after putting Dusty's horse in the officers' stables that Hamley was worried about what he should do with his guests. It was Sunday afternoon, warm, and he could hardly expect them to be cooped up all day. He did not want them to be allowed to wander around and see too much. Dusty could hardly expect to be allowed to do so, not as an officer of light cavalry, the scouts of the army. There were too many things a keen-eyed, intelligent young man could see, even if he did not mean to, too much he could learn by just looking around.

Hamley was torn between a desire to offer no offense to Dusty, who was trying to help a regular officer out of trouble, and his military training, which did not allow an enemy officer to wander about and see whatever there was to see.

Realizing the problem his presence must be raising for Hamley, Dusty offered a suggestion that they see his men to their quarters. They were walking toward the tented lines where Billy Jack and Unwin would stay, and just passing the mess hall, when a fat, grinning man stepped out. He stood looking at the approaching men for a time, the grin growing broader. Removing the white apron from around his waist, he came forward, hand held out.

"Howdy, Cousin Billy Jack."

Billy Jack didn't look any more cheerful at the greeting, although there was a twinkle in his eyes as he replied. "Why, howdy, Cousin Bendigo. Ain't seen you in a coon's age. Say, how come you all in the Yankee Army?"

There was no anger in the question, just mild interest. Cousin Bendigo's grin grew even broader. "Waal, it's a long story. You know what I'm like when I've had a couple of Taos Lightnings. Anyways, I'd just paid off from cooking for a dude who was hunting out West and went out to get a couple of snorts under the belt afore I joined the Texas Light, thought Ole Devil'd want a good cook. I got on my hoss and headed out. Must have got lost, so I took me another snort to kinda clear my head. It sure worked. When I got to thinking about it again, I found I'd joined the army. Only it was the Yankee Army. Didn't figure it made much difference who I cooked for through the war, so I stayed on."

Hamley saw a chance of getting rid of Billy Jack for the period of his stay. "Take a day off, Sergeant Shandon, take care of your cousin and the soldier. See they're made comfortable."

"I'll do that, Major," Bendigo answered. "Come on, Cousin Billy Jack."

"Billy Jack!" Dusty's voice cut across the inquiries after different kin that were being exchanged by the two cousins. "I know there's no place like Texas, no cavalry in the world to touch the Texas Light, and that we run the best damned troop in the Texas Light. But you don't go telling the Yankee soldiers that, especially after *you've* had a couple of shots of Taos Lightning."

"I'll remember, Cap'n," replied Billy Jack, looking even more mournful and sorrow-filled as he turned to go with his cousin.

"A real good man that," Dusty remarked, then a thought struck him. "I wonder if his name's Shandon?"

"Don't you know his name?"

"Well, I'll tell you, Major. I've know Billy Jack for getting

43

on ten—twelve years, but somehow I never got round to asking him what his surname was."

Hamley watched Dusty's face, suspecting a joke, but reading nothing in the young Texan's expression. So he asked something that had been puzzling him all the time. "Is he always as miserable as that?"

"Nope. This's one of his better days."

They entered the house, and Hamley was about to take Dusty to his quarters, when the Texan stopped and looked with some interest at a set of large double doors that led off from the big entrance hall. From behind the doors he heard a familiar sound, a sound that would have drawn his attention anytime. It was the ringing clash of steel against steel, the sound made as swords crossed. Hamley could see Dusty's interest and offered an explanation:

"It's the fencing school. We started it in almost every place we could. This is just about the best location we've had since the beginning of the war."

"Would my visiting it be in order?"

Hamley frowned, not being sure if such a visit was advisable. It would most probably be all right. If only the Third Cavalry regiment officers were present, there would be neither trouble nor danger, for they all approved of what Dusty was doing. However, there might be some of the volunteer officers visiting, and that could prove dangerous to Dusty. A chance wrong word or action could lead to a challenge, and the young Texan could be killed in it. Hamley remembered the way that gun came into Dusty's hand. He knew that no man in the Union Army, including the loud-mouthed, long-haired scout, James Butler Hickok, could equal such speed. There was only one snag. If a duel was caused, swords, not pistols would be the weapon, and Hamley doubted whether the young Texan even knew how to hold a dueling rapier.

Still, a visit to the fencing school would be a way of keeping Dusty occupied and away from anything that he might be able to use later in his campaign against the Union Army. So against his better judgment Hamley agreed to take Dusty to the fencing school as soon as they had washed and tidied up from the ride.

Dusty settled down in his new quarters with no great worries. Still not eighteen years old, he was a seasoned campaigner and long used to making his home wherever the fortunes of war found him. The room was larger than his own back at the Texas Light Cavalry headquarters and better furnished. There were two beds in it, and Hamley indicated the one farthest from the door.

"Would you take that one, Captain," he suggested. "I'd feel safer if you did."

Dusty did not argue with the arrangement. He was always a light sleeper, more so in time of danger, and he was in danger right now. There would be danger to him until the time when he returned to his own people; it was something he accepted without worry.

Unbuckling his gunbelt, Dusty laid it on the bed, then stripped off his coat and shirt. Unwin and Hamley's striker made their appearance carrying water and towels, then left to bring along the box that contained Dusty's best uniform, swordbelt, and other gear.

Hamley could not help but be struck by the incongruity of this situation he found himself in. He and Dusty were of the same race, the same people, yet they were enemies and at war with each other. Dusty's gunbelt lay on the bed; the next time they met, those bone-handled Colts might be throwing lead at him. Then Hamley thought of the meeting between Billy Jack and his cousin and wondered how many other such meetings had occurred, with more tragic results, throughout the bitter years of the Civil War.

They washed and tidied up and went to the fencing school to pass the time until a meal was prepared for them. Unwin put Dusty's gunbelt in the box and got out the uniform to prepare it. His captain was not going to appear before the Yankee Army unpressed and unpolished if Unwin knew anything about it, so he prepared to clean and shine every bit of brass and leatherwork and get a glow on the hilt of the Haiman saber ready for when the court convened the following morning.

The fencing school was formed in what also served as the main dining room or dance hall, depending on which was needed. The furniture was cleared out except for a few chairs and tables at the side of the walls. The tables were littered with fencing gear, masks, and swords. Several Union Army officers lounged around watching the two men in the center of the floor. One of them was Dailey; Dusty saw that, even with the fencing mask the man wore. The other was a slim, fast-moving, dark and swarthy-looking man, who handled his sword with the air of a master. He was obviously only playing with Dailey, for suddenly he redoubled the speed of his masterful attack, driving the young officer before him almost to the wall. Then a fast lunge, and the button-tipped rapier bowed gracefully as it pressed just over Dailey's heart.

Stepping back, the man removed his mark and looked at the young lieutenant with a mocking sneer on his handsome face. He stroked the pencil-thin mustache that graced his sneering top lip and remarked, "It's a pity they don't teach you professional soldiers how to use a gentleman's weapon at West Point."

The jibe stung Hamley and he snorted angrily. "The rapier's all right for a dancing master. But a cavalry man needs a weapon he could use from the back of a horse. Like a saber, there's a weapon for you."

"Really?" sneered the dark man, still mocking and contemptuous. "I haven't been privileged to witness any saberwork by either side yet. How about a few passes with the rapier, Hamley?"

"No thanks, Montreigen."

"Then how about you?" Montreigen asked, looking at Dusty. "Captain, isn't it?"

Dusty looked right back, guessed Montreigen's rank, but did not say so. His voice was an even, yet biting, drawl. "It is, *mister.*"

"Major, New Hampstead Volunteers." Montreigen's face flushed slightly as he made the correction. "How about showing us if the Confederate Army has more skill than the Union in one style of fighting."

The words held a sting to them, but Dusty did not lose his temper. He looked at the rapiers and saw they were using slip-on buttons, so there would be no risk to him. The man was probably trying to humiliate Dusty before the watchers. His words bit back at Montreigen faster than a sword thrust:

"Which kind of fighting did you have in mind, Major? We seem to have held you in most of them."

There was a chuckle at this, even from the Union men who were watching, for Montreigen was liked no more than was his commanding officer, General Buller. The man was a swaggering New Orleans bully and a master with a rapier. They thought his skill with the rapier would show the soft-talking Texan one style of fighting the South could not equal.

Taking the fencing mask from Dailey and slipping it on, Dusty held out his hand to take the rapier offered him. He tested the balance of it, and behind the mask he was smiling.

Montreigen was a New Orleans master, but Dusty was not exactly a beginner himself and had learned, was still learning, from a man who once ran one of the finest fencing schools in the old city of New Orleans, but was now serving in the Texas Light Cavalry.

Montreigen studied the way Dusty lunged toward him, holding the rapier with the point down. Then adopting the classic fencing posture, the swarthy man flourished his sword and said, *"En garde!"*

Instantly Montreigen made a fast lunge, meaning to show Dusty as a bungling beginner and make him the laughing stock of the watching men. His blade was met and parried; it took a fast move to prevent himself being touched by the point that flickered out at him. It took Montreigen just three fast passes of arms to know that here was a man who could handle a rapier in the classic old New Orleans style. The man's fast attack was set by one just as good, the two moving with an effortless skill that told the difference between a man who was good and an expert. Watched by the other officers, the bout went on, lunge, parry, riposte, they came so fast the eye could barely follow.

Montreigen suddenly sprang back and lowered his point to the ground. Dusty stopped his lunge and came to the guard position, smiling behind the mask. He saw the annoyance on Montreigen's face as the swarthy man removed his face mask. The man was seething with anger at the way he'd been fooled by Dusty's pose as a beginner and at the chuckles of the onlookers.

"Captain Fog," Dailey whooped in delight. "You've handled a sword before."

"I'll confess I have," agreed Dusty, watching Montreigen all the time.

"I seem to have undercalled you, Captain," remarked Montreigen. "Suppose we try without the masks. It always bothers me."

"Any way you want, Major."

Dusty dropped his eyes to the floor as he spoke. It was pure luck, or perhaps instinct that made him do so. What he saw warned him that another attempt on his life was planned, a subtler attempt than Packard's way. Montreigen's boot toe moved forward and pressed down as he lifted his rapier, pushing the protective button from the tip of the blade. Once more the rapier was a deadly weapon, not just a sporting implement. This was to be the next try upon his life.

The smile stayed on Dusty's face, but it did not reach his eyes anymore. The prudent thing would be to point out that missing button, but it would tip Montreigen's hand, warn him that Dusty was aware of the danger. The next try might be something less detectable.

It appeared General Buller wanted Dusty out of the way badly and that either he or his men had been shrewd enough to know the fencing school would attract Dusty. If Packard's try failed, there was Montreigen ready on hand to make another attempt. The swarthy Volunteer major knew it would be easy to trick Dusty into a fight, or perhaps force a duel on him. This way was the safer, a friendly bout with the button-tipped rapiers, only there was an unfortunate accident. During the bout the tip must have slipped from Montreigen's rapier. A fast pass, a thrust, and Dusty Fog was down, dead or too badly wounded to give evidence at the court-martial. No one would be able to prove it was other than an accident. Montreigen must be one of Buller's best and most trusted men to be taking such a chance.

Actually Montreigen was as close to Buller as any man ever got. He was a New Orleans dandy, down on his luck and always short of cash. He was also wanted for a murder in the old city and now worked for Buller, trying to instill the social graces into the general.

With this thought in mind, Dusty did not mention his missing button. Montreigen would apologize about it and be free to try some other trick. It would be best to get it over with right now. The man was tricky, most likely a professional duelist, well versed in every dirty trick of the game, but Dusty knew a trick or two himself. He watched the triumphant sneer on Montreigen's face and adopted the correct stance. There were nudges and whispers among the watchers as the two men faced each other. A keen anticipation ran through the crowd. They expected a good show now, for they knew how good Dusty was.

"En garde!"

Montreigen immediately started a fast attack designed to prevent anyone seeing the missing button until it was too late. Dusty was compelled to concentrate entirely on defense for a time, fighting a savage protective battle to keep the lethal point from pricking his flesh. The sneer on Montreigen's face broadened, his eyes gleamed. The reward General Buller had offered to the man who put Captain Fog out of the way was as good as in his pocket.

The blades hissed and clashed, and Montreigen was forced to slack off his fast but tiring attack. Instantly Dusty's hands flickered, and Montreigen found that he was no longer facing a right-handed fighter. The rapier was now in Dusty's left hand, not just held in the left hand but handled completely left-handed. Dusty was transformed, and the sudden change of styles threw Montreigen completely off balance. In his time Montreigen had met left-handed fighters, but never one who could change from right to left in such a manner and so completely.

Dusty's ambidextrous prowess stood him in good stead right now. Montreigen was confused by the sudden move and was unable to adjust himself to the change. Before the other man could set a defense against Dusty's style, a fast attack began. Dusty forced home his attack like lightning. His rapier tip seemed to encircle and wind around the other blade, then with a wrench Dusty tore the rapier from Montreigen's hand, flipping it into the air. It came down point first, and the crowd let out a concerted gasp as the rapier stuck in, quivering.

"No button!" Hamley growled, moving forward, suspicion showing plainly on his face.

"An accident perhaps?" Dusty inquired, face showing nothing of what he felt. "That so, Major Montreigen?"

"A most regrettable accident," replied Montreigen.

Plucking out the rapier, Dusty went and picked up the button, slipped it on the tip firmly, then handed it to Montreigen. Coolly Dusty dropped the tip of his own weapon and repeated the move Montreigen made, pushing the button from his weapon. He knew Montreigen was watching him. Then holding the unbuttoned, dangerous weapon in his hand, Dusty looked at the other man, their eyes locking.

"Try again, Major?"

There was no sound throughout the room as all eyes went to Montreigen. Not one of the watchers saw Dusty's move and wondered what was behind the challenge. Of all of them only Montreigen knew. A bead of sweat trickled down his face, and at last he shrugged.

"No more for today, thank you."

With that he walked to a side table, lay his rapier on it, picked up his coat, and left the room. There was a moment of silence, then Dailey laughed and stepped forward.

"I'll try a few passes, Captain Fog," he said.

Dusty did not accept the challenge right away. He bent and picked up the button, then slipped it onto the tip of the rapier. The other men looked at each other, and Hamley moved forward.

"That happened twice," he growled.

"Why sure," agreed Dusty. "Like Major Montreigen said, a most regrettable accident. I reckon we'd best try the training sabers, don't you?"

With Montreigen out of the way, Dusty relaxed and spent a most enjoyable afternoon in the fencing school. He proved to the others that he was as adept with the saber as he'd been with the rapier, and by the time they broke up to dress for dinner, he'd made many friends.

The entire situation was bizarre, Dusty realized as he washed and dressed for dinner. He was in the presence of his enemies, yet these men were also his friends. They'd played at fighting all afternoon, and the next time they met there might be no play, but just deadly earnest fighting. Yet neither they nor he felt the slightest animosity toward each other. The feeling was one of mutual respect, for they saw in him a master of their trade and he saw them as brave and good soldiers who were relaxing before going out to perform their duty.

The dinner was a lively meal, the talk ranged from horses to the comparative merits of the Colt army and Dragoon revolvers. It was much the same as the conversation in any Confederate mess, the small talk of soldiers. Dusty felt relaxed and at home in the company, and even though his uniform was of a different color, he was one of the men at heart.

The subject of the missing rapier button was not mentioned until just before he and Major Hamley turned in for the night. The major was sitting on the edge of his bed, stripping off his shirt, when he looked at Dusty.

"Do you think Montreigen losing the tip was an accident?" he asked.

Dusty's eyes were mocking. "Don't you?"

Hamley did not reply for a moment. Then he grunted. "Buller's taking a big chance pulling a deal like that. I know who signed that letter to you, so does he. They'd break him in a moment if they thought he'd . . ." The words tailed off as Hamley saw he was saying too much. "The Union Army's not behind any of this."

"I know that," replied Dusty. "Don't worry, none of this will get back to my people. I'd like to see Buller, though."

Hamley smiled. He could guess that any meeting Dusty Fog had with General Buller was likely to prove dangerous, if not fatal, for the general had almost wished such a meeting could be arranged. Hamley was a career officer and had no time for men like Buller, who were using the sacred ranks of the army to forward their own ambitions.

Dusty removed his skirtless tunic and hung it over the back of a chair. The tunic had been the subject of a lengthy and heated discussion in the mess after the meal. The Union officers were not able to decide if it was a good thing or not. Dusty was satisfied that the uniform was the best possible for casual wear and so wore it.

He made no more mention of the two attempts on his life, for he did not wish to embarrass Hamley. The major was acting as his host, and Dusty did not wish to ask any leading questions that might put Hamley in the position of having to criticize a superior officer. They both knew who was behind the attempts and why they were being tried, so they did not need to discuss them. Dusty got the idea, from odd scraps of conversation, that Buller was far from being liked or respected by the other members of the Union Army. He also got the feeling there would be considerable relief in certain high-up army circles if Buller's teeth were permanently drawn. Dusty promised himself that if the chance presented itself he would personally attend to the teethdrawing.

"I hope Billy Jack and Unwin're all right," he remarked as he climbed into bed and lifted the army Colt from his left holster.

"They are," Hamley replied, laying his gun on the chair by his bed. "I went to check just before we came up here. They were playing poker with the sergeant-major and most of the top three-bars."

Dusty felt relieved. Billy Jack, despite his appearance, was no fool. He was a fast-thinking, fast-acting, intelligent man, and a fighting man from soda to hock. A product of the Texas range country, Billy Jack had cut his teeth on the butt of a Walker Colt and grew up fighting bad Mexicans or Indians. The end result was a man who was well able to take care of himself, and Billy Jack could do just that. He was not the sort to be easily forced into a fight, or provoked into anything rash. If he was pushed into a corner, he could take care of himself. Dusty doubted whether Buller's men would bother with Billy Jack until Dusty himself was safely out of

he way. The two Confederate soldiers were safe as long as
Dusty was alive—and he intended to stay alive for a long
time.

"Did you hear about the Packard *hombre*?" Dusty inquired just before Hamley put out the light.

"Yes," replied Hamley, looking at Dusty with some interest. "His skull's fractured and he'll never be the same again.
How did you manage to throw him like that? I've never seen
a trick like it."

Dusty laughed. The tricks Tommy Okasi taught him often
affected people the same way, for it would be many years
before the secrets of jujitsu and karate were widely known
in the Western world.

"It's a wrestling trick I learned from a good friend. Reckon
it works."

"Yeah," agreed Hamley, blowing out the lamp. "I reckon it
does."

With that they settled down to sleep. Dusty pulled the
sheets and blankets up and lay on his side, facing the door,
his gun in his hand. Even in sleep he must be prepared for a
further treacherous attack from the hirelings of the evil man
he was going against. Just before he went to sleep, Dusty
wondered how General Buller was going to take the news
that two attempts at removing him had failed and that one
of Buller's picked men was now in the hospital, badly injured.

The courthouse of Moshogen Town was solemn and foreboding as Dusty waited to give his evidence the following
morning. The main courtroom presented a grim scene,
which not even the blue uniforms of the assembled army
officers, the glinting, shiny hilts of their swords, the high
polish to their buttons could dispel. The usual Sunday
clothes of the town inhabitants, such as attended the court,
were missing for once, the army having taken over.

Inside, at a long table, sat the five presiding officers, a
brigadier general, two colonels, and two majors from other
Union Army units. There was also the law officer from the
judge advocate's department, present to assist the board in
any legal difficulty. Also from the department were the two
counsels, Meadows for the prosecution, looking cold and
hard as befitted a man about to break another; and Silvain
for the defense, a thin, worried-looking man, knowing how
little chance he had of getting Lieutenant Cogshill from this
even with his life.

The young lieutenant stood rigid, trying to hold his face
expressionless, but the strain was leaving its mark on him.
He wore his best uniform, his swordbelt with the sheathed
sword lying on a small table behind the president of the
court, Brigadier General Chambers, a noted cavalry and Indian fighting officer and an old friend of Ole Devil Hardin.

The court was silent as the charges were read out. They
sounded damning in the extreme, and every eye was on
the straight-backed young officer who might soon be await-
ing the firing squad. Due to Packard being incapacitated

hrough an injury, as the prosecution counsel put it, his evidence would have to be read from his official report and sworn statement. It put the defense counsel in a spot, since ae'd hoped to cross-examine, but there was no chance of it now, for the post surgeon doubted if Packard would ever be able to talk or think rationally again, even if he recovered rom his "accident."

The evidence of Packard's statement was damning in the extreme. It was also a pack of lies, with just enough half-ruths to make it hard to break. Buller's own lawyer worked very hard to get such a strong and convincing story, but the end product justified the effort. On the strength of it and without any strong evidence to prove otherwise, Cogshill was guilty of leaving his command in the face of the enemy, and of failing to obey the orders given by his commanding officer.

Silvain's face grew longer and more troubled as he listened to the evidence, for there was no chance of questioning the witness. Things looked bad for Cogshill, and two enlisted men from the Volunteers did not help. They so obviously knew nothing at all about the business of their testimony that neither defense nor prosecution could make anything from them.

"Call Captain Fog!"

Every eye was on the door of the room as it opened. There was a low rumble of talk, checked instantly by the president of the court. The men privileged to be in the courtroom looked at this small, immaculately dressed young man who entered. They all wondered if this could really be the Captain Dusty Fog of whom they'd heard so much. He looked young, very young, although he was every inch a soldier. For such an official occasion Dusty wore the correct uniform, skirted tunic of cadet gray, with buttons and gold collar bars gleaming. The black swordbelt with attached pistol holster, cap box, and combustible-cartridge case, was polished to reflect the scene, the hilt of the Haiman saber glinting in the light. He was as smart as any Union Army man; his striker had seen to that.

Dusty halted in front of the table and saluted the court.

The president looked up without showing any sign of recognition:

"You are Captain Dustine Edward Marsden Fog, Texas Light Cavalry, Army of the Confederate States of America?"

"I am, sir," Dusty answered, and was sworn in.

"Captain Fog." Meadows stepped forward as he spoke. "You led the raid on the Moshogen Bridge?"

"No, sir. I commanded the troop. The actual attack on the bridge was made by my second-in-command, Lieutenant Blaze. I was on the other side of the river, in the woods, and, with my sergeant-major, attended to the destruction of the bridge."

"You say you were on the other side of the river, Captain," barked Meadows in a tone that put fear into witnesses throughout the East. He indicated a well-drawn map of the area, which was on a large blackboard to one side of the court. "I take it you mean you were concealed on the northern side."

"Yes, sir, in the woods."

"Was no search made of the woods, then?"

"No, sir. Lieutenant Cogshill suggested it, but the major refused, saying the Northern side was Union-held country and was safe."

"I see," growled Meadows. "And you were within so close a distance that you could hear what was said—and still remain undetected? Come now, Captain Fog. Is that likely?"

"It depends on how well the horses are trained. Our mounts are trained not to make any more noise than necessary. The wood offers good thick cover and we took extra care that our horses did not make any noise. It was an awkward moment when the lieutenant suggested searching the woods."

"Didn't you expect a search to be made?"

"One always expects as much luck as could normally be on the cards. I hoped there would be no search made."

Meadows snorted. "And if a search had been made?"

"That doesn't come under the province of this court, Major Meadows," the president put in.

"You have my reports of the attack, sir," Dusty said, as

Meadows snorted once again. "Also the report made out by Lieutenant Blaze after the fight."

The president was watching Dusty and holding down a smile. It hardly seemed more than a couple of weeks before that he'd stood in the church in Polveroso City and watched Dusty christened. The boy had grown into a soldier such as the general wished was under his command.

"Tell us in your own words what happened," Meadows ordered.

"The Union troop crossed the river, but instead of forming up guards and taking their post they were lined up. At the same time I was moving toward the edge of the woods by the bridge ready to move as soon as Mr. Blaze drew the troop away. In accordance with the battle plan I had arranged, Mr. Blaze made his charge toward the bridge; then, on being fired upon, turned and pretended to run. The Union troop followed, as I'd hoped they would, allowing myself and my sergeant-major time to blow up the bridge."

The men were all professional soldiers here, with the exception of the few Volunteers who were present. None of the regulars needed any more explanation of the destruction of the bridge; they could guess how it was done.

"Did Mr. Cogshill go with the troop?" Meadows asked, leaning forward to give point and emphasis to the question.

"He followed it."

"Did he obey the orders given by his superior officer—or didn't you hear that part of it?"

"What orders?" Dusty answered. "The major appeared to panic—"

"Object to that remark, demand it be struck from the records!" Meadows barked out the interruption savagely.

"On what grounds?" the president asked.

"Major Buller's actions are not under question."

"Confine yourself to answering the questions, Captain, not giving opinions," warned the president of the court.

"Yes, sir. I heard no official military order given. Mr. Cogshill followed the troop up the slope."

"*Followed!*" Meadows bellowed. "You say he followed the troop. He did not obey the orders given by Major Buller?"

"What orders?" Dusty came back evenly. "I could hear what was shouted with fair accuracy. There were no orders unless 'Shoot 'em' or 'Get them,' classify as orders in the Union Army."

"But Mr. Cogshill hesitated before following Major Buller, even in the absence of a formal command?"

"He did. And so would I in his position. His place was to defend the bridge, not to be taken in by a worn-out old Kiowa trick that wouldn't fool a green one-bar fresh out of military academy."

"We're not here to establish what you would or wouldn't do, Captain, nor to listen to your views on military tactics, profound though they may be. Confine yourself to answering the questions," Meadows snapped.

"My apologies, sir," answered Dusty.

"You said Mr. Cogshill hesitated before following his commanding officer?"

"No, sir. I said he hesitated before leaving his place of duty."

"Don't split hairs with me, Captain!" roared Meadows. "You said 'hesitated.' "

"Yes, sir."

"Thank you, Captain. What happened when Mr. Cogshill reached the top of the slope?"

"Mr. Cogshill saw myself and my sergeant-major and came back to try—"

"You mean he left his troop in the face of the enemy?"

"To come back and try to prevent our blowing the bridge, sir."

"He turned tail from a fight and came back—"

"Not exactly, sir," Dusty interrupted. "My troop was out-numbered by the Volunteers. He came back to face odds of two to one. Even when wounded in the shoulder, he was trying to press home his attack. We were compelled to knock him from his horse before we could get clear of him."

There was a rumble of talk through the court, instantly checked by the president. This was a far different-sounding story from the one Parkard's evidence implied, and for the first time there was a gleam of hope on Silvain's face.

For another half hour Meadows put Dusty through a gruelling cross-examination but nothing could shake the story, and at last Dusty was dismissed and Billy Jack called in. Meadows studied the miserable, slow-looking Billy Jack and opened a savage onslaught on him, trying to tangle his evidence. That was where Meadows made his mistake and was met by a defense as stout as Dusty's and just as unshakable.

Hamley came toward Dusty, two tall men in foreign-looking uniforms following him. "Captain Fog," he said. "I'd like you to meet Colonel Sir Charles Houghton-Rand and Colonel Baron Ulrich von Dettmer."

Dusty drew himself to a brace and shook hands with the two men. Houghton-Rand was a medium-sized, spare-looking man, tanned and hard looking, yet his mouth looked as if it would smile easily. Von Dettmer was tall, his hair cropped short, his face scarred with the saber cuts that told of his class. The two men appeared to be interested in Dusty's tactics, and they talked about cavalry matters until Billy Jack made his appearance followed by the men from the courtroom. Billy Jack's was the last evidence, and the court was cleared while the board considered the case and reached their decision.

Excusing himself, Dusty went to meet his sergeant-major and wondered how Billy Jack could manage to look even more mournful at this time. Dusty wondered how the cross-examination went.

"How's it feel, Billy Jack?"

"Fair," drawled the miserable one. "I won me two hundred dollars at poker last night. Got real lucky."

"Sure, real lucky," agreed Dusty. "There's only one thing wrong that I can see."

"What's that?"

"It's Union money; you can't spend it when we get back."

The two talked on, then separated, and Dusty went to join a group of the Third Cavalry officers he'd met the previous night. They were silent and untalkative as they waited for the order to return to the courtroom. It was a grim and solemn business, waiting to see the result of the court, and none of the men felt much like making small talk.

The court was recalled soon after the men trooped back into the courtroom. The president of the court and the other officers were in their places, Cogshill once more standing before them. Before General Chambers, on the table, lay Cogshill's sword; it would either be returned to him or broken in the next few minutes. The young lieutenant stood rigid, trying to hold his face expressionless and immobile.

There was hardly a sound in the room. A man moved in his seat, and there was a squeak that echoed loudly in the unnatural silence. A man sniffed and it rang out like the bellow of a cannon. Then not even those sounds were heard as the president of the court rose to his feet and cleared his throat.

"Lieutenant William Kirby Cogshill," he said in a hard voice that told nothing of which way the verdict had gone. "It is the finding of this court that your actions at the Moshogen Bridge were correct and that you are to be exonerated from all blame. Also that all charges against you are proved false and will be struck from your record."

With that the president of the court lay Cogshill's sword with the hilt facing toward him. The courtroom was suddenly full of noise. Men moved forward to gather around and congratulate Cogshill. He stood as if he did not believe his ears while his swordbelt was buckled on. Then he turned and looked about him. His eyes went to the man who had saved his life, and he forced his way through the crowd toward Dusty Fog. Smiling shyly, he held out his left hand to Dusty.

"I can't thank you enough for coming, Captain Fog," he said, and winced at the strength of Dusty's grip. "I'm sorry I have to shake with my left hand. As you see, my right is out of action."

There was no bitterness in the way Cogshill spoke of the wound Dusty had given him, and the warm smile robbed the words of any sting. He could feel no bitterness toward the small, soft-talking man who'd come, at considerable risk to his own life.

"I hope you'll soon be well, mister," replied Dusty. "

shouldn't think a forty-four ball through the shoulder is a pleasant companion."

Hamley came over, beaming with delight, and congratulated the young officer, then turned to Dusty. "On behalf of the officers of the Third Cavalry I would like to offer an invitation to a regimental ball, Captain Fog. Your company will be much appreciated."

"When, sir? I have to get back to my own regiment."

"Tonight."

"Then, thank you, sir. I'll be pleased to accept," replied Dusty, for there was no chance of his getting back to the Confederate lines before morning. "And now I'd like to get into a more comfortable and sensible uniform."

Hamley laughed; he'd been one of the chief objectors to the skirtless tunic in the previous night's discussion. They walked away side by side followed by admiring glances from the junior officers of the Third Cavalry. Yet the admiration was not directed at the man in the Union blue uniform but at the small man in cadet gray.

The big hall of the Third Cavalry headquarters was cleared of all signs of the fencing school for the ball. The walls were decorated by the regiment's flags, guidons, and captured Confederate colors. The regimental band were on a raised dais, dressed in their best uniforms and looking unusually smart. The officers of the regiment were all in their best clothes, and there was an exceptional smartness about their appearance, more so than an ordinary ball appeared to call for. The ladies of the regiment were all dressed in their best, as were the visitors, mostly officers from other regiments stationed nearby, but with a fair sprinkling of the upper class of Moshogen's social set, the mayor and the bigger businessmen. It made a gay and brilliant scene, the dresses of the women and the shining metalwork of the men.

For all of that there was an air of expectancy about the place. Dusty could feel it as he made his way among the officers, exchanging small talk with them. He could not make out what the excitement was over; there did not appear to be anything unusual in the ball so far, and the Third Cavalry were not so recently from the battlefront to make this their first ball for some time.

Dusty was no dancer; he could perform the steps but needed to be forced hard before he would do so. He much preferred to stand and watch the others, leaning on the bar, a drink in his hand, with the other bloods. He stood by the bar now, a mint julep in his left hand, a relaxed look on his face as he listened to the unmarried and unattached officers around him passing comments about their companions who were lucky enough to have female company.

It was much the same sort of scene as would be shown at any Texas Light Cavalry ball, only the color of the uniforms was different. The same groups formed, the same sort of action went on, even the same tunes were being played, and around him the same laughing talk of things military, the exchange of stories, the ever-present chatter as the young bloods waited for a chance to dance.

Two men entered the big end doors of the room, although the party at the bar did not notice them. One was Montreigen, wearing his full uniform and looking even more mocking and handsome than ever. By his side stood a huge, bloatedly fat man in the uniform of a brigadier general. He was a fat man, but he was not happy fat; his face was somehow piglike, and there was a mean, vicious look about him. His eyes, small for so large a face, went slowly around the room and came to halt on the small figure at the bar, the man in the cadet-gray uniform. The fat man nudged Montreigen, who looked at the bar and nodded. Then the two started forward across the floor toward where Dusty Fog stood talking with a group that contained Colonel Cogshill and the two military observers.

It was unfortunate that Dusty had been talking about the trick that drew the Volunteers from the bridge.

"Well, I tell you, I'd never have tried it against regular soldiers. But I allowed the Volunteers likely hadn't done any Indian fighting and they might fall for it—"

"What's this Confederate prisoner doing here?"

The roaring voice sounded over every other noise in the room. The band stopped playing and the talk all died away.

Every eye went first to Dusty Fog, then to General Cornelius Buller. Dusty did not speak; he looked the big general up and down without any great interest.

Colonel Cogshill's face darkened in sudden anger at this breach of etiquette, but he controlled his features and held his voice even as he replied:

"Captain Fog is the invited guest of my regiment. He's no prisoner, but here under cartel."

"Cartel?" Buller spat the words out coarsely. "You damned regulars think war's a fool game. If he's here in that uniform, he's a prisoner, and I'll thank you to have him disarmed, ready to be escorted to the nearest prison camp."

"Gentlemen!" Cogshill's one word cut like ice across the angry murmur that rolled up from his men. He was aware that the two foreign observers were trying to look away and avoid taking notice of Buller's breach of good manners.

"Get it done, Cogshill," Buller growled. "Or I'll have Montreigen here do it for you."

Montreigen's face lost its supercilious sneer for an instant. He knew Dusty Fog would never give up his sword without a fight and Montreigen remembered the last time he crossed blades with the small Texan. The swarthy man was no brave when he failed to hold the advantage, and he did not hold it now. He did not relish a fight with Dusty Fog, not when watched by hostile men who would prevent any unfair play.

Cogshill's face was flushed red with suppressed rage. His honor, the honor of his regiment and his country, was at stake here. He could not disobey a direct order given by a brigadier general, even one that should never have been made. On the other hand he could not bring himself to disarm this young Texan who had come to give evidence that had saved his son's life. Cogshill knew that Grant or Sherman would never allow this and would release Dusty as soon as they heard, but the damage would have been done. There was the certainty that Buller did not intend to let Dusty reach the prison camp alive.

"That's an order, Colonel!" Buller snarled. He'd learned early that rarely would a regular officer disobey a direct order.

"Then I protest the order," Cogshill snapped back.

"What order is being protested, gentlemen?"

The soft-spoken words brought the attention of every person in the room to the two new arrivals who stood at the door. One was a middle-sized, stocky, bearded man wearing the uniform of full general and who Dusty recognized as U. S. Grant, commander in chief of the Union Army. The other man, the speaker, was a tall, thin civilian. A man wearing a sober black suit, white shirt, and black tie. A man with a thin, intelligent bearded face. Dusty bit down an exclamation of surprise as he recognized the man from sketches and pictures he'd seen. It was President Abraham Lincoln, the supreme head of the Union. They came forward, Lincoln looking mild, but Grant was beard-bristling with rage.

"What order is being protested, gentlemen?" Lincoln repeated as he came to the party at the bar.

"General Buller wishes to take Captain Fog a prisoner, sir," Cogshill replied, stiffening to attention.

Lincoln ignored Grant's angry grunt and turned to Buller. "A mistake, Cornelius?" he asked. "You did not know how Captain Fog came to be here, I suppose."

"It was a mistake," growled Buller, making the only reply he could. He felt Grant's eyes on him and knew his time in the Union Army was running out. His hatred of Dusty Fog rose even higher.

Buller turned to the barn and snarled an order for a drink of whiskey, and Lincoln nodded to the others. The band started to play again and talk welled up, but it was more subdued. Some of the enjoyment was gone from the ball now and the men drew away from Buller, leaving him standing with Montreigen clear of the rest.

Dusty and the young officers started talking once more. The talk was slightly strained and he turned it to hunting. Then the men around him stiffened up, and he found General Grant by his side.

"Are you Ole Devil's kin, Captain?" he asked.

"Nephew, sir."

"My compliments to him when you get back," Grant

runted, then saw the way Dusty was looking around the room. "Is something worrying you?"

"Just wishing I'd a couple of troops of the Texas Light here now, sir."

"You don't need protection, Captain." Grant sounded huffed at the implications of further danger to Dusty's life.

"I know that, sir," replied Dusty, grinning broadly. "I was just thinking of the haul we could take back with us."

Grant scowled at Dusty, then looked at the people in the room. Then he threw back his head and roared with laughter. "Boy, when the war's over, there'll be a place and commission in the Union Army for you."

"Thank you, sir," answered Dusty. "There's only one thing, though."

"What's that?"

"You haven't won yet."

For a moment Grant's beard bristled, and the men around Dusty prepared to duck, for the commander in chief was known to have a quick temper. Then a twinkle came into Grant's eyes and he began to laugh. Repeating his request that Dusty greet Ole Devil for him, Grant moved on to talk with the senior officers.

The ball went on, but with a more sober aspect, which was not entirely due to the presence of President Lincoln and General Grant. Buller was alone at the bar as Montreigen joined in the dancing. The big man drank whiskey after whiskey, and his face grew more mean and vicious at every moment. Then as the band came to a stop at the end of a tune, he raised his voice.

"I want to give you a toast!" he bellowed, raising his glass. "To the Union and the downfall of those lousy rebel traitors."

There was complete silence all over the room, not a move from the crowd as every eye went to the small man in the cadet-gray uniform of the Confederate Army. Dusty did not move and his face never changed expression, but he put his glass deliberately on the bar top. Then man after man put his glass down, and Grant barked out:

"There's no call for that, Buller."

"Man's a damned bore," Houghton-Rand said *sotto voce*, but it carried around the room.

Dusty made no move, but his face was hard and there was a tightness to his lips. Any man who knew him would have warned Buller that the time was coming to hunt for the storm shelters, for Dusty Fog was getting riled. For all that Dusty held himself in control; only the way his clenched right hand tapped against his side showed any sign of how he felt. He was pleased that his cousin Red was not along. Red Blaze would not have stood for Buller's actions; he would have swung a fist.

The music started once more, but the bandmaster was having trouble keeping his musicians' attention, and the dancers were not more than half trying to keep up a festive appearance. The officers of the Third Cavalry were seething with rage, and the general feeling among them was that Buller should have the door indicated to him and then be thrown through it.

Buller poured another drink down his throat and moved along the bar to stand before Dusty and look down at him.

"So you're this Captain Fog, are you?" he snarled, the hatred dripping from his whiskey-loaded breath. "Just what I'd expect for a lousy corpse-robbing rebel."

Dusty's cheeks showed two spots of color, but he held his voice. "I'm an officer of the Confederate States Army, *sir*. I'd like that remark explaining."

"My brother was carrying nearly two thousand dollars and a new navy Colt. Neither were on his body when he was brought in."

"And you're saying I took them?" Dusty's voice dropped to little more than a whisper.

"That's just what I'm saying."

"Mister, you're a liar!"

Dusty's right hand knocked the catch from his holster flap as he spoke, for in Texas no man used the word *liar* unless he was willing to back it with a Colt. Buller's face went almost purple and his fist clenched. For a moment he thought of smashing his fist into the small Texan's face, but even in the throes of whiskey fury he was able to think sensibly. He

66

remembered what had happened to Packard, a man skilled in the fistic arts. If Packard did not stand a chance against the small Texan, Buller knew just how much chance he would stand.

"I took a new navy Colt from Packard, a real fancy weapon for a man to be carrying," Hamley put in. "And he lost nearly fifteen hundred dollars in a poker game the night he was promoted."

"So?" Buller snarled.

"The gun was engraved with your brother's name, and that's a lot of money for a hired man to be losing."

"And I couldn't use Union money, mister. Unless you're telling us your brother was carrying Confederate money."

Buller's temper was boiling over, but he was still not fool enough to try outright violence against Dusty. He knew that Hamley was probably telling the truth and he'd only accused Dusty to make trouble. He'd lost the exchange of words and his rage boiled over.

Dusty wanted no trouble, nor did he want this scene to carry on. He started to turn away, but Buller caught his arm and turned him.

"Take your lousy hand off me!" Dusty's voice sank to just over a whisper, and the concentrated fury made the big man drop his hand.

"Why you short-grown runt!" Buller snarled. "If you was taller I'd—"

"Hire somebody to do something?" Dusty finished for him. "You've tried twice and I took both of them."

"Why you . . . !" Buller began, then words failed him and he drew back his fist. Instantly his arm was caught in a vise-like grip and he turned to meet Cogshill's cold eyes.

"That's enough, Buller. Get out of here. Now!"

Dusty stood very still. At his side his right hand was held flat, thumb bent over, palm and fingers stiff and rigid for the *nkite,* the four-finger piercing hand of karate. In another instant the steel-hard fingers would have driven into the fat stomach, doubling Buller in agony and helpless for the next attack Dusty would launch. Dusty was almost beyond controlling his anger, but the interruption prevented him from disgracing himself. The few seconds' pause gave Dusty time to regain his control and stop his temper.

Buller could see the end of his career in the army. He could read it in Grant's angry gaze, in the looks of the crowd. There would be a polite note asking him to resign, which if not accepted would be followed by a point-blank order to do so. It would be the end of his hopes, his dreams of social acceptance as an officer of the army. Worse, he would be an outcast and even such doors as had previously been opened to him would slam closed now. His full rage turned on Dusty Fog, and for the first time in his life Buller spoke without caution.

"Why, you lousy, short-grown rebel scum," he snarled. "If you were man-sized, I'd squash you under my boot heel."

Like a whiplash Dusty's reply cut back, biting through Buller's rage and lashing at him. "If the general will waive question of his rank, I'll waive my natural reluctance to fight someone who is obviously no gentleman."

It was the one thing capable of making Buller throw off the last vestige of self-restraint. The words struck home, biting into his ego. More than anything Buller wanted to be known as a gentleman; every move he made was to that end.

"Well said, well said," growled Houghton-Rand from behind Buller, and that brought the rage boiling out.

Buller's face turned a deep purple, and for a moment Dusty thought the man would have a stroke. The fat hands clawed up to tear away the cravat and pull the neck of the shirt open. For an instant Buller was on the verge of throwing himself bodily at Dusty, but sanity prevented him from doing so. This was the man who had beat Packard, sent him to the hospital with a broken head. Buller had every cause to know how tough Packard was and that he could not handle Dusty Fog. There was only one alternative, a duel.

Then Buller's mind started to work fast. Cold steel was out. Montreigen could not handle the Texan with a blade, and Buller knew how skilled a performer the swarthy man was. Buller was but a poor performer with any kind of sword, having neither the grace, speed, skill, nor balance to make a skilled fencer. A mounted duel was out of the question, for the Texan was born and raised in a country where a horse was more than just a means of transport and where a man could ride as soon as he could walk. A mounted duel would be fatal—and not for Dusty Fog.

That left Buller only one chance, and it was one he relished: pistols. He was not better than fair with a handgun and was sure Dusty was better than just fair. However, there was trickery, and Montreigen knew every trick in the book. Pistols were Buller's only hope of surviving a fight with Dusty Fog.

"I'll waive anything if it'll make you fight," he snarled.

"Gentlemen," Grant put in, growling the words out. "That's enough. There'll be no dueling. Captain Fog's here—"

"Your pardon, sir," Dusty interrupted politely, his tone respectful. "General Buller has cast doubts on my honor and my personal courage. It cannot be overlooked, since these gentlemen have all heard. I demand satisfaction on the field of honor."

Grant was in an awkward position. Dueling was forbidden by law, but he knew that the law was frequently flouted by serving soldiers. The Southern gentleman was one who refused to follow the law and chose the field of honor to settle his differences. Hoping for guidance, Grant glanced at Lincoln, but the president was talking to the mayor of Moshogen and making sure he kept his back to the trouble, leaving the army to sort out its own internal troubles.

So the decision lay on Grant's head. Dusty Fog was completely in his rights and Buller never more in the wrong. Grant was far from being a fool; he knew why men like Buller joined the Union Army. That might have been why he made the decision he did. He was putting Dusty Fog into danger, but he knew Dusty was well able to handle the trouble. If the duel was allowed, the Union Army would lose a dangerous enemy one way or the other. Grant doubted if Dusty would be the one to fall—strangely the thought gave him some satisfaction.

"Very well, Captain," he growled. "Buller, send your seconds to wait on Captain Fog."

Dusty was presented with a problem. He did not wish to ask one of the Third Cavalry officers to act for him in a duel against a member of their army, even though he knew they would do so willingly. He turned to the two military observers and asked if they would act for him. Houghton-Rand and von Dettmer could see the position Dusty was in and agreed to be his seconds. Telling Buller they'd wait for his seconds in the library, they left the room. Buller, followed by Montreigen, left the room, and the band started up once more, but all the festivity was gone from the air now, and the ball started to break up soon after.

Montreigen and another Volunteer officer came into the room soon after and found Dusty waiting with his seconds. Buller was not present; he'd told Montreigen how he wanted to fight and left the New Orleans duelist to think up some plan to give him the edge. Buller's decision to use pistols gave Montreigen an idea, a dirty trick and one that would ruin Buller socially but should keep him alive. It would be the end of him in the Union Army, but he was finished with the army anyway. Buller hoped his money would shield him from worse happenings, and he expected to be able to live down the distaste other people might feel at his methods.

"General Buller wants us to state that he does not use the sword," Montreigen said, getting down to business without any small talk. "He wishes to fight with pistols."

"That is to our principal's satisfaction," answered von Dettmer, a trifle haughtily. He was a Prussian and had fought in duels, but to him a duel was only correct when edged weapons were used. However, Buller could select any kind of weapon and condition as long as it was fair to both participants in the duel.

"Further, as there is no chance of getting a working pair of dueling pistols at such short notice, the general suggested each man uses his own Colt revolver. That will be fair to both participants, and each revolver will have only one percussion cap. The next to fall under the hammer. That will be satisfactory?"

"Quite satisfactory," Houghton-Rand replied, glancing at Dusty.

On the face of it the terms were more than satisfactory, for Houghton-Rand knew how good Dusty was with a revolver, having spoken to young Cogshill on the matter earlier. With his own weapon in his hand Dusty would have a decided edge in the duel, more so than if both men were using a strange dueling pistol, the vagaries of which they did not know.

"Then tomorrow at seven o'clock," Montreigen went on. "General Buller's a busy man and doesn't want to waste any more time around here."

"Very good," barked Houghton-Rand, annoyed at this implication that Buller must win on the following morning. "If that's all, Major, we'll return to the ballroom. After you, sir."

The following morning several men gathered in the orchard behind the house. Grant was not to be seen and Colonel Cogshill was in charge of the affair. Besides Dusty and Buller there were the four seconds: Billy Jack, the post surgeon, and a couple of Volunteer officers. Buller stripped off his coat, his fat shape packing and straining at his thin silk shirt. He stood scowling, watching Dusty remove his tunic and unbuckle the gunbelt, then take the right-hand gun out. Dusty passed his tunic and gunbelt to Billy Jack, who accepted them, looking unhappy and far more worried than he felt.

"Make sure there's only one cap on that gun. Montreigen," Buller scowled.

Houghton-Rand opened his mouth to protest at this breach of etiquette, but Dusty shook his head. Reversing the bone-handled Colt, he held it out toward Montreigen as the man came up.

"Take a look, Major, although I'm not willing to allow you to touch the gun."

Montreigen smiled. It was a sneering, mocking smile, yet there was something furtive in it. He looked down at the reversed Colt and saw there was only one percussion cap in place; the other nipples were clear and the gun could only be fired once.

Houghton-Rand made the obvious suggestion, but Dusty

shook his head. "I'll treat General Buller as if he were a gentleman."

The British colonel smiled; this youngster was a cool hand. Those words bit into Buller like a whiplash and made the man almost shake with rage. It would do his shooting no good at all to be in such a temper. However, Houghton-Rand wished he could make sure there was only one percussion cap on Buller's revolver.

The two men were called together and stood back to back. Each held his revolver in his right hand, muzzle pointing to the sky. Cogshill stepped forward and asked. "Is there no chance of you forgetting this, gentlemen?" There was no reply. "Very well. I will say commence. As you step off, I will count to ten. Then both turn and fire. Is that satisfactory?"

"It is," Buller growled.

"Why sure," agreed Dusty.

"Commence!" Cogshill snapped, and the two men stepped forward. "One! Two! . . ."

There was sweat running down Buller's face as he stepped out the paces. Yet there was a look of triumph on his face. He drew back the hammer of his Colt and faintly heard the click of Dusty's revolver come to full cock. The count was going on, and at each word they took another step.

"Five! Six! Seven!"

"Look out, Dusty!" Billy Jack yelled out a warning, forgetting military formality in the urgency of the situation.

Buller was turning on the eighth step, swinging around to stand sideways, left hand on his hip, right bringing the revolver down into line, adopting the stance Montreigen taught him. The long-barreled Colt crashed out, the bullet ripping by Dusty's head, for in his hurry Buller flinched his pull and his shot missed. The recoil kicked the gun barrel high and Buller cocked back the hammer, apparently forgetting there was only supposed to be one chamber capped.

At the sound of the shot Dusty turned fast. Not for him the fancy duelist's stance; there was no time. He knew Buller was not making a mistake; the revolver Buller held was fully capped. Dusty knew this and acted on it. His turn ended with him ready, feet apart, legs slightly bent and body thrown forward to offer a smaller target. The army Colt swung down to line, held centrally with his body and only waist high. It was the stance of a frontier fighting man, a man used to shooting and hitting a man-sized mark in less than a second, starting from the leather. The gun roared while only waist high, flame lashed from the barrel, behind the heavy .44 bullet. Through the whirling powder smoke Dusty saw Buller rock over backward and crash to the ground. Even as the big man fell, his gun crashed and the bullet tore into the turf by his side.

Montreigen slapped at his holster, knocking open the top and gripping the butt of his revolver. He was slow, real slow, when faced by a man who had learned his gunfighting in the West. Billy Jack dropped Dusty's tunic and belt; his right hand stabbed down and brought up his Colt. Before the dropped articles hit the floor, Billy Jack sent a second bullet into the reeling man, then covered the other Volunteer officers.

Cogshill and the surgeon ran to Buller's side, bending over him. They stood up and Cogshill took the fallen revolver, looked at it, then came to Dusty, face working angrily.

"On behalf of the Union Army I apologize to you, Captain Fog," he said, showing the revolver was fully capped. "General Buller cannot apologize for himself. He is dead."

Dusty did not reply. He turned and went to pick up his jacket, pulled it on, then strapped his gunbelt around his waist and set it right. He turned and walked back toward the house, where breakfast was waiting for him.

The president of the United States walked with the captain of the Confederate States Army as Dusty made his way to where his party were waiting to be escorted back to their own people.

Lincoln looked at the small man by his side. Man? A mere boy in years, but a man full grown for all of that.

"I'd like to apologize once more for all that happened here, Captain Fog," he said. "I and General Grant would have given anything to avoid it."

"Apologies aren't needed, sir," replied Dusty. "There are

men like Buller on both sides. Whoever wins the war's going to have to watch them real careful. They're dangerous in war, but they'll be more so just after it. I don't hold anything against the rest of you and have told Colonel Houghton-Rand and Baron von Dettmer so. They agree the Union Army behaved correctly and honored their side of the agreement I came under. Any blame for anything that happens lies with General Buller, and he's beyond our reproof."

Lincoln felt relieved, for he'd spent a worrying night thinking of how the attempts on Dusty must look to the foreign observers. Now he could see Dusty had cleared up any doubts the British and Prussian officers might hold.

"You'll see your own leaders know this?" It was a statement really, not a question, for Lincoln knew Dusty would do so.

"Yes, sir, although Uncle Devil will know without being told. There are hotheads who might like to make political capital out of it. I will see that the true facts are known."

They walked in silence for a few moments, then Lincoln asked, "Why do you serve the Confederacy, Captain? Do your family own many slaves?"

"We don't have any, sir. Got a few colored folks down in the Rio Hondo country, but I wouldn't call them slaves. Uncle Devil made the decision. He leads the clan and he decided it was our duty to fight for the South. We followed him on it."

"You wounded young Cogshill at the Moshogen Bridge?"

"Sure."

"I suppose you were trying to kill him?"

"Waal, we were riding fast at each other. There was no time for fancy shooting. I just shot to stop him killing me, wasn't bothered where I hit him so long as I hit. Reckon you could say I was trying to kill him."

"And if you see him in action, you'll try to kill him once more?"

"Likely," replied Dusty, thinking along the same lines as Lincoln, and a half smile playing on his lips.

"And yet he would have been shot without your evidence to clear him. That is certain." Lincoln's gentle drawl went on, a smile on his face that made him look dependable and likable. "Would it have made any difference if we'd shot him, or if he was killed by you?"

"None in the end, I suppose. Except for his honor."

"His honor," Lincoln mused, watching Dusty's face. They were nearing the waiting party now. "You risked your life to save his, yet you would kill him tomorrow if you saw him in action. It's a strange world, isn't it, Captain?"

Dusty nodded. "Yes, sir. Makes a man think how futile war is."

PART TWO
THE UNION SPY

CHAPTER ONE

"Lynch her! Hang her! Kill the Yankee spy!"

The hate-filled voices of the mob rose high into the night air, shattering the peace and turning hideous the air of the quiet Southern town. The light of flickering torches showed off the faces of the men and women who headed for the big old house and yelled hatred to the skies.

At the gate of the house's garden a small, frail woman in her early fifties watched them come, standing stiff and erect, showing neither fear nor any other emotion. Through the war she'd served the Union well, doing her duty as she saw it, fighting the only way she could. Now it appeared the truth was known, although how she could not guess, and the price must be paid. The people who formed the mob were her friends and neighbors. Only the day before, some of the women were at her home taking tea with her; now they were here with this hate-filled mob, screaming for her blood.

Nearer came the mob, the rumble of their hatred, the most savage and ugly sound in the world, grew louder as more and more people joined the bunch and heard that Elizabeth van Bruwer was a Union spy.

The woman felt a shiver run through her and tried to restrain it as she stood waiting for them, a slender, small figure with a spotless white cap on her head, a sober, plain black dress that extended to her feet. There was no escape for her; the Confederates took all but one tired old horse for service with the army. So, with no hope of escape she came to face them. The van Bruwers were a sturdy stock, the men having served their country in every war. She would do nothing to disgrace the family name.

The mob advanced, and they were almost at the house when hooves thundered loud and three horsemen rode between the woman and the crowd. The horses turned, rearing and pawing the air, bringing the mob to a halt for fear of their iron-shod hooves. Then the horses settled on all four legs and the riders faced the crowd. A stop came to the mob, brought about by the determined look of the three men who faced them. There was menace on the face of the tall, lean, miserable-looking sergeant-major at the left and on the face of the freckled, pugnaciously handsome, red-haired lieutenant at the right. There was more than menace in the cold, gray-eyed stare of the small, young-looking captain in the center. It was he who spoke, his voice cool, commanding, and firm. The sort of voice a man heard—and obeyed.

"All right. Hold it up, right there!"

All eyes were on the small Confederate Army captain, and he looked back at them with cold contempt plain on his face.

Some of the mob, a good part of it, were the sort Dusty Fog expected to see on such an affair: louts, town bullies, and loafers. The sort of men who avoided taking any part in the war other than sitting at home, being fiercely patriotic but making sure they took no risks themselves. They were the kind who would be on hand for any kind of hell-raising that offered but the slightest risk. Yet there were others present who definitely did not look to be the kind to become involved in a lynch mob. Honest citizens, the better-class people, law abiding, the sort who did not go to war because they were too old, urgently needed at home, or unable through ill health. The small woman must have done some real bad act for such people as those to be wanting to lynch her.

It was one of these better-class people who spoke, a man who knew Dusty by sight. "That's Elizabeth van Bruwer, Captain Fog," he said.

"So?" inquired Dusty, lounging easily in his saddle, but watching the crowd.

"She's a lousy Union spy, that's what's so," yelled a voice well hidden in the crowd.

"The war's over, mister!" Dusty's voice was not loud, but the words carried to every member of the crowd.

"Over?" gasped the man who'd spoken first. "What happened, Captain?"

"We called off the killing," Dusty replied, thinking back to the scene at the Appomattox Courthouse when General Robert E. Lee had brought to an end the long and bitterly fought Civil War.

The South was defeated by economics, not on the fighting field, for the poorly armed, gray-clad warriors would have fought on to the last drop of their blood if given the order. It was just that the South could no longer afford to fight, so Lee took the only sensible way out and brought an end to the useless killing.

At Dusty's words silence fell on the crowd, the lynching forgotten. The war was over, the South beaten, their way of life gone forever. Peace brought the crowd no happiness, only the numb, raw, aching hurt of defeat. Slowly the crowd began to break up, men and women heading for their homes. As they went, someone began to sing the Confederate battle song:

> *I wish I was in the land of cotton,*
> *Old days there are not forgotten,*
> *Look away, look away . . .*

Dusty rode his horse forward and halted the man who first spoke to him, recognizing a citizen with whom he'd done some business for the Texas Light Cavalry. "How'd you know the lady's a Yankee spy, friend?"

"A man told us so, a man at the tavern."

"That's a kind of slender thing to hang a woman over, isn't it?" asked Dusty. "Did he offer to prove it?"

"Showed us some papers that said he was working as an undercover agent for the Confederate Army. Said he and his friend were going to arrest her. Then the talk got going that she should be hung."

"Who started it?" Dusty asked, knowing the Confederate

Army's undercover agents were given nothing to identify themselves. "The lynch talk, I mean."

"I don't know for sure."

"What did the man who told you about her look like?"

The man thought for a moment. "A big, heavily built man, with a heavy black beard that hid most of his face. I think he'd been a sailor."

"How'd you know that?"

"He reached out for a drink across the bar and I saw an anchor tattooed on his wrist. His friend called his attention to it and he covered it up quickly."

"What'd the friend look like?" asked Dusty.

"A tall, thin man, pale-faced and with a small beard. He's got the meanest pair of eyes I've ever seen, light blue, they were and expressionless. Looked more like a snake's eyes than snake's eyes do," explained the man. "I think we all lost our heads. We know all her folks are Yankees, and she's a strange one, living here all alone except for her two servants. I don't know what come over us, but there's a lot of us lost kin in the war."

"Killing her won't bring them back," said Dusty. "Leave her be, friend. The war's long over and there's too much work to be done now to bother about old hates."

Dusty turned his horse to ride back and join his friends as they sat their horses guarding the woman. He thought of going to see the two "undercover agents" and finding out what proof they could offer, if only to satisfy a theory he'd formed just before the Appomattox. He decided not to bother; there was no need for him to get the proof of his theory now; the war was over. He sat on his big black horse and watched the crowd going off, the torches discarded and burning out in the dust of the street. There would be no more trouble again that night.

Elizabeth van Bruwer looked at the three men who had saved her. Dusty Fog, Red Blaze, and Billy Jack—she knew them all by name. The Union Army would have given plenty to capture any of them, particularly the small captain called Dusty Fog. Only one thing in her spying activities did she eel any shame at, something connected with the three men who just now saved her life.

"Was I you, ma'am," Dusty said, looking down at the woman, "I'd pull out of here until folks forget this. We'll escort you to the town down the trail a piece."

"Thank you, Captain," she replied. "This is my home and 'm too old to leave it now. I'll stay on here and hope that people will forget it. Would you care to come in and take a meal?"

"Why sure, thanking you kindly, ma'am. We haven't sat to a table in a week, been riding steady since the Appomattox, warning our people the war's over, so there'll be no incidents when the Yankees move in."

The three men left their horses in the almost empty stable behind the house, attending to the animals before they made any attempt to feed themselves. The big old house was empty and deserted, only a couple of rooms being in use. Miss van Bruwer led the three Texans into a candle-lit dining room, where two scared-looking Negroes were cowering back against the wall. They showed more fear as the three men entered, for this was an uncertain time and they'd heard the noise outside.

"Be seated, gentlemen," she said, waving them to seats, then turned to the two Negroes. "Ezra, Mandy, we have three guests. Make a meal for them."

The three Texans took seats and Miss van Bruwer urged her two servants out of the room, into the kitchen. She came back and took a chair at the head of the table, sitting prim and erect on it. She saw Dusty looking at her with some interest.

"So you're Miss van Bruwer," he said. "I was thinking of coming to visit you when we got word of the meeting at Appomattox."

"Really?" the woman smiled. "I didn't know my fame extended to the Texas Light Cavalry. Did I make a mistake that told you what I was doing?"

"I guessed, ma'am. There'd been a powerful lot of information leaking out from this area, and you was the only person who'd been present at *all* the leaks. It all figgered to

me. I learned your background, how your kin were aboli-
tionists and went north just before the war. How you stayed
on and was real hospitable to any soldier who came your
way."

There was no animosity in the way Dusty spoke, just plain
admiration. He'd made use of information gained by the
Southern spies Belle Boyd and Rose Greenhow on more
than one occasion and did not see there was any moral
objection to the North using spies.

"I came near to capturing you once," Miss van Bruwer
remarked.

"When was that, ma'am?" asked Dusty, and his two
friends looked interested. They knew there'd been times
when the Yankee Army came near to catching them but
could not think of any time they'd been involved with the
woman.

"Do you remember when the Union held this town, before you drove them back?" she explained. "You came
down here to meet a renegade firearms dealer and collect a
consignment of arms."

"Why sure," agreed Dusty. "It cost me three good men,
but I got out and took the arms with me."

"You say you nearly got us captured that time, ma'am,"
Red went on, for the three men were all friends. "How was
that?"

"I put it down to bad luck, meeting the Yankee patrol,"
Dusty drawled.

"It was bad management, not bad luck. The dealer came
here as soon as he got word of where you would meet him
and to collect payment for betraying you. But you didn't go
to the place where you were supposed to meet him and
slipped out of the trap. You'd have got clean away with it if
you hadn't run into a stray patrol."

"So they were waiting for us?" mused Dusty.

"Yes, but you didn't go where you said you would meet
him."

"That's right, ma'am," agreed Dusty. "I didn't, fact being
never aimed to go where I arranged. A man who'd sell arms
to the enemy wouldn't play square with anyone. So I worked

FLINT
IF HE HAD TO DIE, AT LEAST IT WOULD BE ON HIS TERMS

Get a taste of the *true* West, beginning with the tale of *FLINT* FREE for 15 Days

Hunted by a relentless hired gun in the lava fields of New Mexico, Flint *"settled down to a duel of wits that might last for weeks...Surprisingly, he found himself filled with zest for the coming trial...So began the strange duel that was to end in the death of one man, perhaps two."*

If gripping frontier adventures capture your imagination, welcome to The Louis L'Amour Collection! It's a handsome, hardcover series of thrilling sagas by the world's foremost Western authority and author.

Each novel in The Collection is a true-to-life portrait of the Old West, depicted with gritty realism and striking detail. Each is enduringly bound in rich, Sierra-brown leatherette, with padded covers and gold-embossed titles. And each may be examined and enjoyed for 15 days. FREE. You are never under any obligation; so mail the card at right today.

Now in handsome Heritage Editions

Each matching 6" x 9" volume in The Collection is bound in rich Sierra-brown leatherette, with padded covers and embossed gold title... creating an enduring family library of distinction.

ut which way he'd come and met up with him. I thought he ooked surprised when he met us four miles from the place where we was supposed to be. He'd got his face covered nd I couldn't say."

"What'd he look like, ma'am?" asked Red.

"I never saw his face either. He came to this room, as by rrangement with one small lamp lit and he stood well back xcept for when he came to get his money. He wore a flour-ack mask," she answered, then, seeing the look on Red's ace, smiled. "I have no reason to lie, young man. A man olaying both sides of the fence must not take any chances of eing known. He would have sold me out as easily as any ther person, if he could have done it safely. All I know is hat he's tattooed on his right wrist."

"What kind of tattoo, ma'am?" growled Red.

"I'm sorry, young man. But he—"

"We saved you out—"

Red Blaze was always a hotheaded young man who both aid and did rash things without thinking. His inborn good oreeding revolted at his words, and it was to his credit that le stopped speaking even before Dusty's angry interruption ame.

"Red. That's enough. We'd have helped the lady, no mat-er who she was. She owed nothing for doing it."

Miss van Bruwer smiled at Red as he stammered his apol-ogies for his lack of manners. "It's all right. I know how you must feel. There's no real reason why I shouldn't tell you. The man gave no loyalty to the Union and I owe him noth-ing. The tattoo was an anchor. I saw the flukes of it as he reached out for the money. It was the first time I'd seen an anchor tattoo since I left New England. When—"

Dusty's face lost the relaxed, friendly look and became hard. He sat up in his chair and snapped, "Red, go down to the tavern, take Billy Jack, and bring me those two men who should be there. One of them's big and bearded, the other thin, got a smaller beard. They likely only checked in today. Fetch them back here."

Red and Billy Jack came to their feet and went fast. When Dusty Fog's voice took on that grim note, there was no

standing around and asking fool questions. It was time t
obey and obey fast. Miss van Bruwer watched the two go
then turned to Dusty, a question plain in her eyes.

"Might I ask what that was all about?"

"The two men who started the lynching talk going, ma'am
The men who told folks you were a Yankee spy. I want t
see them."

From the way he spoke, Miss van Bruwer guessed Dusty
did not aim to say any more about the men and she did no
press him. Dusty was worried for her sake. The anchor tat
too might have been a sheer coincidence, or it might be the
renegade arms dealer getting rid of someone who knew
about the identifying mark on his arm.

"That man you knew, he'd got the tattoo?" he asked.

"Yes, I remarked on it and he became angry, said I'd imag
ined it. Just at that moment Mandy knocked to tell me Gen
eral Handiman's aide had arrived, and the man left hur
riedly."

"Lucky," Dusty said softly.

"What do you mean?"

"If he hadn't, you'd likely be dead now. You're maybe the
only one who could identify the dealer. I couldn't, or any o
my men, because it was dark when we met."

Red and Billy Jack returned half an hour later from the
tavern. "They've gone, pulled out," Red remarked. "Left as
soon as the mob started. We went to the livery barn and
found they'd brought their horses there earlier, then fetched
them and gone out of town by the north road. Went out a
piece after them but they'd got too much of a start. Who
were they?"

"I don't know for certain, thought I'd warn them off."

Miss van Bruwer watched Dusty's face and she almos
guessed the truth, fantastic as it first looked. Her gentle
voice cut in, just as the food was brought and set on the
table in front of the three men.

"What do you intend to do about the traitor, Captain
Fog?"

"Nothing, ma'am," replied Dusty. "The war's over now
Long over, as far as I'm concerned. The OD Connected's

ping to need a powerful amount of work doing to it, setting back paying again, and there'll be no time to waste trying to find one man with an anchor tattooed on his wrist. We likely couldn't do it, even had we the time, and we haven't."

Red grunted. He, too, knew there would be little or no time to waste in search for a man on such feeble evidence. There were many men with anchors tattooed on them, and one could easily be lost forever. The man was just one of the many who saw war as a chance to line their pockets. The sort who would side with one faction, yet deal with the other and betray both. Such a man was to be despised, killed if caught at it, but Red knew it was too late to catch the man now. It was like Dusty said, hard work in plenty awaited them at the OD Connected and there was no time to be wasted on a revenge hunt.

All through his young life Red was never the sort to hold a grudge. He'd pitch in and fight any man, but after the fight, was just as willing to shake hands and be friends, even ready to help the man he'd just fought with, if help was needed. So he did not bear the woman any grudge and he, too, remembered how they'd profited by the spying of two Confederate women, so could hold this Union spy no ill-feeling. Right now he was seated in a comfortable chair and a good meal was waiting for him; his thoughts about the rights or wrongs of Elizabeth van Bruwer's actions were put off and forgotten.

The following morning in the early light of dawn Dusty Fog mounted his horse and looked down at Elizabeth van Bruwer. She stood at the gate of her garden, a woman in her fifties, he a youngster still in his teens. Yet each had played a part in the War Between the States, serving as best he or she could. Now the war was over and peace, uneasy peace, lay on the land.

"The war's over!" said Miss Van Bruwer as if she could hardly believe it.

"Yes, ma'am," agreed Dusty, looking at his two companions, who were mounted, and ready to resume their ride back to Texas. "The war's over, and now *you've* got to face

the peace. It won't be easy for you, ma'am. Good-bye—and
good luck."

Touching his hat, he turned the horse and rode away.

She watched Dusty ride off along the street, a small man
between two tall men, but she'd never think of Dusty Fog as
small. Turning, she went back to her silent, lonely house, a
house that would be even more silent and lonely from now
on.

CHAPTER TWO

The war had been over for eight years, and they had been busy years for Dusty Fog. On a mission of importance in Mexico he met two good friends, who now rode with him as members of the OD Connected's floating outfit.* His wartime record was being forgotten as men spoke of him as *segundo* of the huge ranch, trail boss of the first water, town-taming lawman—and the fastest gun in Texas.

Seated in the mayor of Mulrooney's office, Dusty looked at the beautiful Miss Freddie Woods, Town Marshal Kail Beauregard, and Shepherd, a top railroad official. He wondered why Freddie had called him to her office—she was mayor of the town and an old friend from the days when he ran the law in Mulrooney†—on his arrival with a trail herd. Freddie did not keep him in suspense.

"I want you to find a man for me, Dusty," she said.

"Is it important?" Dusty asked. "I've promised the crew to whoop things up for them."

"It's real important, Dusty," Beauregard put in. "I can't leave town right now to get the feller and it has to be done."

"What'd this feller do?" Dusty inquired.

"He killed five Texans," Freddie said, and went on after a slight pause, "one of them was called *Allison.*"

"You'd best tell me all about it," drawled Dusty, knowing the significance of that name and who was following him up the trail.

* Told in *The Ysabel Kid.*
† Told in *The Trouble Busters.*

"All started when Ed Baylor brought the first trail herd in this season," explained Beauregard. "The Magluskey brothers were railroad superintendents and not friendly gents at all. They didn't like Texans, and Mike Magluskey got into a fuss with Ed Baylor. Died of a case of slow. His gun hadn't even cleared leather."

"Which same figgers. Ed's some fast with a gun."

"Like you say, Ed's some fast with a gun. Trouble was Ed left town the following day, headed for home. Two nights after, that's four days back, Joe Magluskey and another man went into the Fair Lady. They stood at the door and started shooting at five Texans who stood at the bar. Young Tim Allison managed to come around and shoot Magluskey before he went under, but the other man got away. I was coming along Main Street as he came out, and we traded shots. He threw four at me. Real curious that."

"What's curious about it?" asked Dusty. "A man coming from a deliberate killing would likely try and shoot it out."

"He'd fired five shots into the Fair Lady and had only one gun."

"Which same makes nine shots, happen you've got the right of it."

"It was right," Freddie put in. "I'd bought a new bar and there wasn't a bullet hole in it. He would check."

"Sure, Magluskey fired off two shots, his gun was there. Six bullets in the men at the bar, one in the bar away from them enough so it couldn't have been caused by a ball going through one of them. It made seven, two from Magluskey and five from the pale-faced dude."

"With the four outside made nine shots he fired. Figgers he wouldn't have time to reload before he lit out. He using a revolver?"

"What else could he be using?" asked Beauregard.

"A Volcanic pistol, they hold the shots, or a sawed-down Winchester."

"Neither, it was a revolver," Freddie answered. "I saw it before I went under a table."

"I never saw a ten-shooter, though," remarked Beauregard. He did not disbelieve Freddie, knowing her to be cooler than most men when there was shooting going on.

"I did," Dusty replied. "In the war. European-made, pin-fire guns. Uncle Devil brought one home with him for his collection. I tried it and didn't like it. A man'd have to like one of them to keep on toting it when he could get a Colt. Mind, they weren't bad guns, as guns go, but they couldn't touch the old army Colt for easy pointing or accuracy." He paused, looking at the others. "You'd best finish it off for me."

"Sure," agreed Beauregard. "He threw his shots fast and he was good with it. I felt the wind of the bullets and it must have put me off. Anyway, he lit out, and by the time I got up, he was gone. I couldn't find hide nor hair of him, and as soon as I saw what happened, I got every man I could lay hands on looking for the killer. We went through every room of every house in town; didn't hardly leave a stone unturned without looking under it. Mr. Shepherd here's head of the railroad and his men did the same with every inch of railroad property. A train left town just after the shooting but we got word ahead and brought it back again, with the train crew watching that nobody got off."

"You didn't find the man?" asked Dusty.

"We didn't. We know for sure he didn't leave the train. The railroad crews didn't like the Magluskeys and don't hold with cold-blooded murder. They made sure the dude wasn't hidden either on a train or on railroad property and he didn't get picked up by a train outside town. He couldn't have been in town the way we searched, and there was no stage out during the night. To make sure, I had men pick each stage up a couple of miles out of town and search them for two days after. Told the guards to hold any man who tried to board them within four miles of town. Nothing came of it."

"He could have pulled out on a hoss," Dusty pointed out.

"He didn't. I sent riders out of town, good men. Besides, he was a dude and not fixed for riding and he didn't go on a horse, not from the Fair Lady. He'd have brought one to the saloon if that was how he aimed to escape. At dawn I had men who could read sign making a circle of the town limits looking for a sign that left about the time of the shooting. No sign of a horseman leaving. And a man isn't going to ride across country, not alone and in dude's clothes. Attract some attention if he did. If he went south, he'd be likely to run into cattle drives, and to the north the Cheyennes are out."

"Looks like you didn't search the town well enough, Kail."

"We searched the town well enough," Beauregard replied. "I've notified every town within two hundred miles, and the town council put a bounty of a thousand dollars on his head. Folks gave their cooperation when they heard who was killed, and I let it be known Clay Allison's coming up trail. That dude couldn't have paid to hide out here."

Dusty agreed with the words. Clay Allison was well enough known to get the required cooperation. Allison was a tough Texas rancher with a penchant for treeing towns and killing Texas-hating Kansas lawmen. He was not the sort of man who would mildly overlook the killing of one of his kin. Under normal conditions Allison's visit to Mulrooney would be carried out with none of the wild hoorawing any other Kansas trail-end town received. Allison liked and respected Freddie Woods and knew that she ran a clean town, so he behaved himself in it. However, if he came and found one of his kin murdered, he would tear the town apart board by board, and Kail Beauregard would not stand by to allow it. That would mean more killing.

Freddie Woods showed once more that she knew men and how they reacted to certain circumstances. "You know what it will be if Clay comes and finds we haven't got the man, Dusty. But if we can tell him you've gone after the man, he'll be willing to hold off until you get back."

That was true enough. Clay Allison and Dusty were friends, members of the select group who wore gunbelts made by old Joe Gaylin of El Paso. They were a select group, the men who wore the Gaylin gunbelts, for the old leather worker would make a gunbelt for only a man he felt was worth the honor. For a man to be wearing a Gaylin belt meant he was someone to be reckoned with, one of the magic-handed group who could draw, shoot, and hit his mark in less than a second. So, if Allison knew Dusty was hunting the killer, he would hold his men in check until he heard the result of the search.

"Look, Kail," Dusty drawled, seeing the difficulties of the search. "If he didn't leave town by rail, stage, on hoss or foot, he must have found something new by way of transport. And I've not a helluva lot to go on. How about a description of the man. He got wings or something?"

"We learned something about the man," Shepherd put in. "I got the section boss, Shamus O'Toole, and we questioned a few friends the Magluskeys made. Shamus can get persuasive when he has to. Apparently one of the men got the idea the dude didn't like the idea of it. The man didn't know what was going to happen, for they turned him away from them."

Dusty smiled, remembering Shamus O'Toole. He could imagine how the questioning took place, punctuated by the thud of hard fists most likely. O'Toole could be very persuasive with his hard fists when he needed to be. "This man who gave you the voluntary information, he describe the dude?"

"He did his best. Said the man was tall, slim, and pale-skinned, with pale blue eyes. Real mean eyes, he reckoned."

"Did the man come in off the railroad?" Dusty asked Beauregard.

"Nope."

"By stage?"

"Try again."

"Born the day before the shooting and aged real fast," grunted Dusty, getting tired of it all. He'd just come off the trail from a hard drive and was in no mood to play guessing games.

"Nope," replied Beauregard, grinning. "He came in by train all right. One that runs on four wheels. A wagon train. At least, that's how he's traveling, with a westbound wagon train. It didn't come into town and it camped about a mile and a half out, beyond that big *bosque* out there. We never even heard anything about them until last night, when a buffalo hunter got to joshing Miss Freddie about how much money she must be making, with his sort, railroad men, trail-drive hands, and wagon train folks all coming into town."

"I hadn't seen any wagon train, so asked him about it. He said there'd been one camped out there on the night of the shooting, found sign to prove it. So I told Kail right away," Freddie put in.

"Sure, at dawn I went out with the buffalo hunter. He could read sign near on as well as the Ysabel Kid. Showed me tracks of one man on foot coming to town. My men must have missed, or overlooked them, looking for sign of a man on a horse. He walked in direct, but took a roundabout line back. That makes me sure it's the one we want. So we want you to go after the train and bring him in."

"How about these Magluskeys? What does the railroad know about them?"

"Nothing much. They did their work well enough, weren't liked, and were under suspicion of dealing in the sale of arms to the Indians," Shepherd replied. "Nothing was proved, although they were thought to be mixed in with a ring who sold arms to the Confederate Army during the war."

It was then Dusty's tenacious memory got what was bothering him, some half-forgotten thought at the back of his mind. He remembered that night when he stopped the lynching of Elizabeth van Bruwer. Remembered the description of the two men who tried to start the lynching. A tall, thin, pale man with a pair of mean, light-blue eyes. Dusty did not mention his thoughts on the matter, it was hardly likely they were the same men. Although a man who dealt with running arms to the Confederacy might still be in the same business, selling to the Indians. It was highly likely he would be running guns still, for he would have a source of supply ready laid on. Dusty looked at the other three.

"So you reckon the man went with the wagon train?"

"Everything points that way," Beauregard agreed.

"They've got a four-day start. Allowing them traveling twenty-five miles a day, they'll be near enough a hundred miles from here, in the Cheyenne country," said Dusty thoughtfully. "A man on horseback'd make better time and catch up with them."

"He will also have to be either brave, or plumb loco to go in there alone," Freddie stated, knowing Dusty would go.

Dusty grinned at her, a grin she remembered from the days when she was trying to keep the town from folding through lack of trade and she'd first met him.

"Why sure. But don't reckon to be going in alone. I'm taking a Comanche with me, and the Cheyenne was never born that could show a Comanche any tricks."

Freddie smiled, looked relieved for the first time since the killings. "You shouldn't talk about the Kid like that."

CHAPTER THREE

The wagons formed a white-topped circle in the bottom of a valley. It made a peaceful sight, a community on wheels, a town going West to the new land and a new home. The sun was sinking and the cooking fires blazed, wafting pleasant smells of food in preparation as they would in homes across the country, except that here the kitchen was in the open, roofed by the sky. Small groups of men gathered, talking as they waited for the evening meal. The groups were made of men who spoke with the hard accents of New England and the Northern states and the drawls of Virginia and the South. Men who eight years before might have been shooting at each other in the war now banded in harmony, all with a common bond, the land to the West.

Seated by her wagon in a rocking chair, an old woman knitted with quiet concentration, unbothered by the hustle and the talk around her. A shadow fell across her, and she looked up at a big, bluff-looking, yet somehow reliable man who stood by her side.

"Evening, Grandma Brewster," he said.

"Evening, Major."

Major Chris Brant, wagon master of this train, paused in his nightly walk, as he always did, by the side of Grandma Brewster's rocking chair. He stood there now, a big, self-reliant man, hard, tough, and capable, yet with a knowledge of human nature that stood in good stead on the long trip West. This was his fourth trip as a wagon master, and he'd taken a mixed variety of people West, but this woman the train called Grandma Brewster surprised him. She was far older than was usual in one starting to go west, a slight, frail-looking woman with a thin, gentle face that always wore a smile. Her passage was paid for, her Conestoga wagon one of the best, and her team as good as money could buy. She was accompanied by an old Negro couple, who cooked for her and drove the wagon. Who she was and why she was making the long and arduous journey to the California coast no one could say. She was going and she made herself useful and no one questioned her as to her reasons.

Almost everyone on the train liked the soft-spoken, gentle old woman. She'd become a kind of mother-confessor for anyone who needed a problem solving or wanted a shoulder to cry on. This was something Brant appreciated, for the women would have brought their little problems to him had not Grandma Brewster been along to listen and offer advice to them. She also helped with any nursing and acted as a midwife when it was called for. She gave her gentle wisdom, told the children stories, and ran a Sunday Bible class for them.

"Everything all right with you?" Brant asked, as he'd done every night of the trip.

"Fine, thank you, just fine. And you?"

"Easy so far. Tracy came in just now and told me there's no sign of the Cheyenne. They're likely further north."

"I'll tell the ladies' sewing circle when we meet later tonight. That young Mrs. Raikes is all a-twitter, sees Indians behind every rock and tree. It should be a relief to her to hear there are none—but I doubt it. That young lady dotes on misery and worry."

Brant laughed. He'd come to rely on Grandma Brewster to keep twittering young wives like Mrs. Raikes out of his hair; it was one of her many self-appointed duties. He was about to remark on the fact when a woman hurried by them, making for a wagon further down the line. She was a scared-looking, painfully thin woman with straggly dark hair and a pinched face. Her thin gingham dress was torn and old, clinging to a figure that bore only the last vestiges of womanhood. She scuttled by, head bowed and eyes on the ground as if afraid someone might stop and speak to her.

There was pity in Brant's eyes as he looked at the woman, and Grandma Brewster shook her head sadly.

"Poor Mrs. Holman," she cried. "I never really disliked anyone until I saw her husband. He's as near a beast as any man could be."

"Yeah," agreed Brant, breaking one of his prime rules. He would never have thought of discussing one traveler with another, not to any other person on any train he took West. Somehow this woman was different. He did not think of her as one of the travelers, but as much a part of his staff as his cook, driver, second-in-command, or scout. "I think we've stopped him mistreating her. I threatened to turn him off the train the next time it happened. Well, I'd best finish my work. Old Joel told me not to be late for my meal."

Brant walked on, greeted by and speaking to the various people who were by their wagon fires, politely refusing invitations to eat with them. The Holman wagon stood in the circle, yet, as always, gave the impression of being separate from it. Mrs. Holman was working on the fire, but there was no sign of menfolk.

Holman was a big, burly brute of a man who always looked as if he needed a shave, even though he took a razor to his face at least once every day. This was surprising in a man who seemed so careless of his appearance. He was a sullen, surly man, unfriendly when sober, mean and harsh when drunk. His drunken treatment of his wife almost caused trouble, and only Brant's stern warning brought an end to the ill-treatment that had roused the other men of the train to anger.

Holman was not liked, nor was his son, a tall, slim, and sullen youth who always wore a Colt in a low-tied holster. It was a significant rig, the lip of the holster cut away to allow easy access to the trigger of the weapon, even as it was being drawn. He also tied down his holster, and in the West they said, "A man who ties down his holster doesn't do much talking with his mouth." Frank Holman spent hours in the practice of fast draws. He was a troublemaker who relied on a gun to back any foul play he created.

There was another man with the Holman wagon. A paying

passenger, it was assumed, for nobody knew for certain. He was a thin, pallid dude who always wore dark-tinted glasses and was disinclined to do work of any kind. He was rumored to be almost blind and was supposed to be going to California for his health.

They were not a sociable group, the Holmans, never joining in any of the fun or activities of the other travelers. Brant watched them early on and found they knew far more about living in a wagon than any of the other families. The very way Holman escaped the pitfalls that trapped many of the other people made Brant suspicious. He did nothing to prove or disprove his suspicions, and by the time the train was settled down to the trail, he'd all but forgotten them.

Brant's walk ended by his own wagon, at the right side of the main entrance into camp. His cook was setting out the plates for the evening meal, and the scout of the train lounged by the wagon side. Suddenly Tracy Wade stiffened and looked toward the rim. He was a tall, lithe young man wearing buckskins and belting an old army Colt at his right, a bowie knife at his left.

"Riders coming, Major," he said.

Brant looked up the slope at the two men who were riding slowly toward the wagons. He frowned as he looked at the men. It was unusual to see a group as small as two men in this country. Occasionally there might be a fast-moving dispatch rider, or an Army scout, but they traveled alone. These two men were none of those kind. They wore a style of dress Brant had never seen this far north and west, the dress of cowhands, Texas cowhands at that.

Brant watched them as they came closer, an oddly contrasting pair in appearance, but each mounted on a big, powerful, and fine-looking horse. The taller rode a huge white stallion, one of the finest-looking horses Brant could ever remember seeing. He was a tall, slim, lithe youngster, his clothing all black, even his gunbelt. The walnut grips of the old Colt Dragoon gun at his right side, butt forward in the holster, and the ivory hilt of the bowie knife sheathed at his left made the only contrast in color against the blackness. His face looked young, very young, and the features were tanned nearly Indian dark.

The other man hardly attracted more than a single glance from Brant. He was small, handsome, young-looking, yet insignificant. It seemed strange that so small a man should be riding such a fine-looking animal as the big paint stallion. The hand-tooled *buscadero* gunbelt with the bone-handled army Colts in the holsters, their butts turned forward for a cross-draw, did nothing to make the boy look more noticeable. Brant hardly gave him a second glance, turning his eyes once more to the Indian-dark boy on the big white.

Tracy Wade stood by Brant's side, a smile playing on his face, as he watched the two men. He'd been surprised to see two riders coming in like this, until he recognized them. Those two could ride anyplace they wanted and were fully capable of backing their decision to do so. They were men skilled with the revolvers they belted and with the Winchesters that were booted under their legs.

"Howdy," greeted the smaller rider, halting his horse outside the camp circle. This was the etiquette of the land, a man halted and waited for permission before riding into a camp.

"Howdy. Light down and take something," Brant, as wagon master, gave the required permission. "Rid far?"

This was also the etiquette of the land, asking for more details than the other men called to give.

"Came out from Mulrooney. I'm Dusty Fog, this here's the Ysabel Kid."

"I'm Major Brant, this's my scout, Tracy Wade," Brant answered, looking Dusty over and wondering if he really could be the Rio Hondo gun wizard.

Tracy Wade supplied the answer to that. He moved forward with his hand held out and a welcoming smile on his face. "Howdy, Lon, Cap'n Fog. Ain't seed either of you in a coon's age."

"Tracy, you ole Kiowa!" the Ysabel Kid whooped. "I didn't know you was riding scout for this train."

"Thought you'd have been jailed years back," Dusty went on, then to Brant, "Mind if we night here, Major?"

"Feel free," replied Brant, thinking how two such young men would make a very useful addition to the fighting strength of the train if they were traveling in the same direction.

Dusty and the Kid left their horses standing by the wagon, attending to the big animals before thinking of their own welfare. They lay their double-girthed Texas saddles carefully on the sides under the wagon, then joined the other men at the Brant fire. The cook brought out two extra plates and filled them with the stew that formed the main dish of most of his meals. Brant watched his two guests as the meal was eaten, wondering what brought the *segundo* of the OD Connected ranch so far out into the wilderness.

"You're a far piece from home, Captain," he said when the meal was done and he'd offered his cigar case to Dusty.

"Man'd say you were right," agreed Dusty, politely refusing the cigar and rolling a cigarette with deft fingers. "Came after you on a chore for the sheriff of Mulrooney County. We're looking for a man."

Before he and the Kid pulled out from Mulrooney, they found Freddie Woods had moved with her usual speed. There were two deputy sheriff's badges and a warrant for the arrest of a man unknown ready for them. The badge, warrant, and a covering letter from Freddie, as mayor of Mulrooney, were inside Dusty's shirt pocket and he did not take any of them out. There were wagon masters who would take a wanted man West with them, at a price, getting them safely through the arms of the law and the dangerous Indian country. Brant did not look like one of that kind. He'd built a reputation of honesty and square-dealing. He was hiring Tracy Wade, who was the Kid's friend, a fellow member of Mosby's Rangers, although that proved little. The Kid possessed a large selection of friends, including a number of badly wanted men.

"Looking for a man?" repeated Brant. That could either mean they were after a fugitive from the law or after him for revenge.

"Sure," agreed Dusty, taking out the warrant and letter. "Got the notion he might be traveling with you."

"We haven't taken on no strangers or new folks since back of the Kansas East Line. Nobody joined us at Mulrooney. Is the man wanted badly?"

"Depends on how you look at it," answered Dusty. "He helped kill five Texas men in the Fair Lady saloon."

Brant was shocked by this. Five killings at one time was going some, even for a wild train-end town. "So you figure he's traveling with us."

"Waal, way we got it, the man didn't leave on hossback, by railroad, or stage. Word has it he was new in town, might have been with you all the time."

"That's possible," agreed Brant, meeting Dusty's eyes with a frank, honest look. "But as far as I know, nobody went into Mulrooney. They were all stocked up with supplies and didn't need anything. Most of the folks aren't rich, and I warned them how the prices in a town like Mulrooney went up in the trail-drive season, so they stayed on by the wagons. We had us a dance, and I can't recollect, offhand, that anyone was missing. Nobody took a horse from the lines— we always keep a double guard when we're near a big town; stops horse stealing. So we'd know if a horse was taken."

"Sign showed a man came in on foot. You weren't more than a mile and a half out, a man could walk it easy," Dusty said. He explained the special circumstances that had brought him after the train. Brant knew Clay Allison's reputation and could see how urgent the situation was. Dusty went on. "Everything Kail Beauregard could learn points to the man being with you. He knew Magluskey back in the East, which makes it more likely he's traveling with your train."

"It also means he'd have to know the country, to make a mile and a half walk in the dark," Brant remarked. "As far as I know, none of my folks ever were out here before."

For all that, his half-forgotten suspicions started to come again. His eyes flickered through the fast-gathering dark toward the Holman wagon.

"Town makes a tolerable amount of light after dark, and noise," Dusty pointed out. "It wouldn't take much finding."

"What sort of a man are you looking for?"

"He's tall, thin, pale, and got real light-blue eyes. Totes one of those ten-shot pin-fire revolvers that came in from Europe in the war. Least, that's the way everything points."

Brant frowned. He thought of Holman's paying passenger. The man was tall, thin, and pale, but Brant could not remember ever seeing his eyes and never seen him with a gun of any kind. In fact Hogan Joubert, the passenger, always said he could not handle a revolver, never learned. So Brant kept his suspicions to himself. The man might be innocent and there was no point in starting Dusty's thoughts running toward a man who might possibly have had nothing to do with the shooting in the Mulrooney saloon.

"It takes a good man to handle one of those ten-shot guns," remarked Brant. "A friend of mine took one from a reb officer he captured and we tried it. Took more handling than an army Colt. You'd best leave it until morning, then ask around the folks. Some of them might know something."

Dusty's reputation and the explanation he'd given for coming after the man caused Brant to give this permission. Dusty was not just after the man for a bounty, or Brant would not have given the word. Dusty and the Kid were not bounty hunters, but others would hear of the reward and its connection with the wagon train. *They* would be bounty hunters, and some innocent man from the train might get hurt. With this in mind, knowing Dusty's testimony on the subject would be accepted, Brant gave his permission.

"Gracias," said Dusty. "We'll night here if we can."

"Be my guest," replied Brant, waving a hand to his wagon.

A group of men came toward the wagon. Brant watched them, wondering what problem was to be piled on him now. The men halted, and a big wide-shouldered man stepped from the others, saluting Dusty.

"Cap'n Fog, sir," he said, voice showing his Deep South origin. "I'm Sergeant Tapley Evans, Virginia Cavalry. These other gents all served the South in the war, and we'd admire for you to come to my fire and talk over old times."

"Be my pleasure, sir," Dusty replied formally. "If you'll excuse me, Major."

Brant agreed to this with a smile. He was an old soldier

himself, as was almost every man on the train. He could appreciate the men of the Confederate Army wanting to have a long reminiscence session with one of the South's heroes. He watched Dusty and the Kid walk away, then saw Tracy Wade following and growled:

"Where do you reckon you're going?"

"Me?" grinned Wade. "I'm a Southern boy myself, so I'm going to join in the fun with the others."

Slightly less then half the grown men of the train were gathered around the Evans fire, and his plump, smiling wife handed out cups of coffee, borrowing cups from the neighboring wagons when her own ran out. Then she withdrew, and a bottle was brought out to make the rounds as stories and laughter started to roll out.

It was the first time all the Southern men gathered at one time in one group. Usually the groups were mixed and smaller. The Union Army men among the Northerners watched the scene with tolerant smiles. There was no animosity in the way they watched the Southern men, and any of them could have joined the circle if they had wished. None joined the group, respecting the other army's feelings. They would have acted in the same manner as the Southern men had a Union Army hero come to the camp. So they stayed by their own fires, watching and smiling tolerantly at this display of old-soldier reunion.

Brant was out visiting the horse guard, and the cook stood alone by the major's fire washing dishes. He looked up as the tall, thin, dark-glasses form of Hogan Joubert loomed up. The Holmans' paying passenger looked to where Dusty and the Kid stood in the center of the group at the Evans fire.

"Who're they, Joel?" he asked.

"Dusty Fog and the Ysabel Kid," the cook answered. He did not particularly care for Holman or the thin man, but he was a talker and liked to gossip with somebody. "They come out from Mulrooney looking for a man."

"What sort of a man?"

"Didn't tell me. I heard them say this feller killed five Texans in Mulrooney. They allow he's with the train and are going to start asking around in the morning, see if they can find him."

Joubert turned on his heel and walked away before the cook could say another word. He kept to the darker shadows and avoided the Evans fire as he went back to the Holman wagon and climbed in. Holman was not inside, being away taking his turn on horse guard, but his wife and son were both in the wagon. The woman sat on a box at the back of the wagon, sewing an old dress and not looking at either of them.

Young Frank Holman sat on the edge of the bed. His gun lay beside him and a cleaning rod showed that he'd been busy working on the weapon. Joubert did not say a word until the youngster strapped on the gunbelt and holstered the Colt, setting it right on his side with meticulous care. Then as Holman holstered his gun and looked up, Joubert spoke.

"You allus wanted to see a good man with a gun, young Frank. Come on here and take a look."

Frank Holman fastened the pigging thong around his leg and stepped to Joubert's side, by the door of the wagon. His mother looked up, her mouth opening to say something, then closing again. There was more than fear in her eyes, but she did not dare speak the words that welled up inside her. This was the moment she'd feared ever since her son was old enough to strap on a gunbelt.

Standing by Joubert, Frank Holman looked out to where the men stood around the Evans fire. Most of them he knew, and they were not fast men with their guns. He knew Tracy Wade was fast, but not exceptionally so and not enough to warrant this sudden interest. Then his eyes went to the Ysabel Kid, took in the old Dragoon gun, and dismissed it as out-of-date, not the thing a real fast man would be wearing. He saw Dusty and would have passed the young Texan by, but at that moment Dusty turned to address a man at the other side of the fire and Holman felt a thrill run through him as he saw the two guns Dusty wore. He knew that a man only wore two guns to make people think he was real good —or because he *was* good.

"Is that him, the small cowhand?" he asked.

"That's right, boy. He's Dusty Fog."

"Dusty Fog." Frank Holman breathed out the words. "You aren't funning me, now, are you, Hogan. A short runt like that being Dusty Fog?"

"Short-growed or not, he's Dusty Fog all right. I saw him in Dodge one time."

Frank Holman bit down his excitement. He was fast with a gun, or his long hours of practice were wasted. His every waking moment that could be spared to it was devoted to the endless practice of fast draws and shooting at the man-shaped target he would draw on a tree or a rock, or anywhere handy. His one ambition was to be known as a fast gun, to meet and kill a man with a reputation. Now fate threw the fastest and best of them all this way. Dusty Fog, the fastest gun in Texas, the man whose roaring guns and chain-lightning draw had tamed Quiet Town and Mulrooney. That was the sort of man Frank Holman dreamed of meeting and killing. That would be something people would point him out and say, "That's Frank Holman. He killed Dusty Fog, Wes Hardin, Ben Thompson, Bill Hickok—" Holman felt his pulse quicken. After Dusty Fog he would strike out and find the other fast men. Soon he would be holding such a reputation that every big town would clamor for his services as marshal. There would be no trouble if he killed Dusty Fog. Brant and the others would never dare go against such a man, one so fast with his gun.

"You'd best steer clear of him, boy," Joubert warned. "He's real fast."

"So am I!" Frank scoffed back, irritated by Joubert's tone. "I never yet saw a man who could beat me."

Joubert knew that the youngster had never faced a man in a gunfight. His tone was aimed at deliberately making Frank go out and face the Rio Hondo gun wizard.

"Shucks, I know you're fast, Frank boy. But I don't think you've got a chance against a man like Dusty Fog."

"You don't, huh?" Frank growled. Nothing could have been said that would make him more determined to go and face down Dusty Fog. "I'll soon show you. I'll bring you his gunbelt."

Joubert watched the youngster loosen the Colt in the holster. There was an evil grin on his face and he removed his glasses. Pale, cold blue eyes blinked at the young man as he started to climb out of the wagon. Then Joubert turned and went to open his box. He pulled the clothes aside and lifted out the revolver that lay hidden. It was a strange-looking weapon to eyes that were used to the hand-fitting, curved butt of the army and navy Colts. The butt of the weapon looked as if it were carved from a broom handle, straight, round, and set at an angle to the working parts of the gun. The hammer was long and bent over the top of the chamber to strike the pin that was fitted to and fired each cartridge. The chamber was big and bulky and held ten .54-caliber bullets.

Joubert hefted the gun with some satisfaction. He'd come by it early in the war and had grown to like its awkward grip and the fact that it held ten heavy-caliber bullets. To his mind this offset the serious disadvantage of the gun: its poor instinctive pointing qualities due to the shape of the butt. That was what had saved the life of that town marshal in Mulrooney. Joubert had tried to fire from waist high and, even after all the years of practice, still could not do so with any skill. There would be no such mistake tonight, Joubert swore to himself. While all eyes were on Frank, he would be able to take careful aim and fire. If there was any blame, it would fall on Brace Holman's head, for the people of the train did not know Joubert owned and could handle a gun.

Checking the pinfire loads, Joubert went to the door of the wagon and climbed, watching young Frank Holman walking purposefully toward the Evans fire and his destiny.

Dusty Fog was relaxed and completely at ease among the men. He laughed at a story one of them just told and was about to top it with one of his own. He forgot, or put aside, the reason for his being here. The man, if he was on the train, might be popular and people would object to his being taken back to Mulrooney to stand trail. It was something he'd have to face when he came to it and nothing would be gained by worrying over it.

"So you're Dusty Fog, are you?"

The voice came from behind and Dusty turned slowly. It was a tone of voice he knew well and guessed any quick movement on his part might start something he did not want right now. He could have guessed what was waiting for him when he turned, and his guess was right. Behind him stood trouble. The young man in the north-country range clothes, the dress of a dandy who looked more like a cowhand than worked like one. That low-tied gun told a man things, happen he'd been around and Dusty Fog had been around. To him it spelled just one thing. A youngster who thought he was fast with a gun and looked for a chance to prove his theory.

Across at the Holman wagon Joubert watched. He could not take a hand until Frank went for his gun and the shooting was decided, but he cocked the heavy old gun ready.

Joubert had been cursing himself for a fool ever since his visit to the town of Mulrooney. He had gone in to buy a couple of bottles of whiskey and relieve himself of the boredom of the train, the sameness of the journey. A meeting with Magluskey was the last thing he expected or wanted. There was no refusing Magluskey's request for help, for the man knew too much about him and Joubert wanted no trouble. All in all Joubert was not sorry when Magluskey went under at the Fair Lady saloon; it meant there was one less man alive who knew how Holman and Joubert made their living.

Having gone in on foot and returned by a roundabout route, keeping to hard ground as much as possible, Joubert had been sure there was no way he could be traced. Yet these two Texans were here and they knew what he looked like. In the morning they would start to look for him. Frank Holman knew Joubert had been into Mulrooney; so did Brace Holman and his wife. Of the three Frank was least to be relied on; he might say the wrong thing. It would be as well if Dusty Fog killed Frank first, then both he and the sabel Kid were shot down. If Major Brant made an investigation, Joubert would be in the clear.

Dusty turned to face Frank Holman, then nodded, never king his eyes from the youngster's. "That's right, friend," e agreed, voice even and friendly.

"They say you're fast with a gun."

"Who do?" asked Dusty, his tones mild.

Frank Holman's mouth hung open and for a moment he as at a loss for an answer. This was not going the way he nagined it would. He'd thought of this situation many times d in it the other man either showed fear at being faced by e terrible Frank Holman or went for his gun immediately d died with it still in leather. Instead of either thing happening he was asked a question and did not know what ply he should make.

"Everybody does," he finally got out.

"Not everybody knows me, or's heard of me," Dusty inted out.

A chuckle ran around the crowd. The men were from an ea where gunfights were not common and did not know hat this apparently harmless talk was leading up to.

"I don't reckon you're fast at all," Frank spat out, riled by e chuckles of the other men in the circle.

"You want to know something, friend," Dusty answered, ishing the other men had not chuckled, reading the anger Frank Holman's face as a result of it. "I don't think I'm fast ther."

Tracy Wade knew the signs, knew what this was leading p to, and knew how little Frank Holman had if he went for is gun. He moved forward to try to stop the trouble.

"This's another man's fire, Frank, and you're not invited it."

By the code of the wagon trains a man's fire was classed his home, and no other man could come to it without king for and receiving permission to do so. The youngster ew the rule but broke it, sure his gunspeed would protect im.

"You keep out of this, Wade," Frank hissed. "This's between me and the short man here."

"Hold hard now, Holman!" Evans barked. "Cap'n Fog's my guest and I ain't having you coming here unasked and insulting him—"

"What's wrong, small man?" Frank interrupted. "You scared or something? Hiding behind the big man here. You yeller or something?"

"Call it that if you like, boy," Dusty replied, but there was a harder edge to his voice now. "All right, you've called me down, run your bluff. Now just drift along and leave us to our talk."

"I go when I'm good and ready!" Holman hissed out the words. "There's nobody here can make me go."

"You're that fast with a gun?" asked Dusty.

"The fastest there is."

"Shouldn't need to go around proving it, then, should you?"

The Ysabel Kid was by nature a suspicious man. It was what kept him alive in the dangerous scouting duties he took on for the OD Connected. So he was not giving his full attention to what was happening near at hand. Ole Dusty could handle three of that boy's sort, happen both his arms weren't busted, and they weren't. So the Kid looked around. In one of his constant glances around the camp he'd seen the thin man talking to the major's cook. He'd watched Joubert go to the Holman wagon, enter, then the youngster came out. Then he'd seen Joubert emerge and caught a glimpse of the gun in the man's hand. The Kid read danger in all this and held his right hand, palm out, thumb hooking into his belt to hover over the worn walnut grips of his ole Dragoon gun.

"I'm fixing to see how fast you really are," Frank Holman warned Dusty, standing with legs bent slightly and fingers spread over the butt of his low-tied gun.

"Waal, I'll tell you friend, I'm not fast at all. It's just that every man I had to kill was slower than me."

"I'm not!"

"I've not met you—yet."

Holman gulped down something that seemed to have blocked his throat. "Draw!"

"Not until you do."

Suddenly there was no longer a small man before olman. Dusty Fog was now a big man, a man who loomed igher and wider than any other man in the crowd. Fear hit rank Holman, and it was fear that drove him to yell, Draw!" once more.

Tracy Wade caught Frank's arm and tried to shove him way from the fire. "Get away from here before you wind up eing killed!"

Frank Holman's temper snapped, driven by fear. He ushed Tracy away and spat in Dusty's face, his hand droping toward his gun.

Dusty moved forward. There was something in his face at scared Holman more than any amount of screaming urses would. His right fist smashed into Frank's stomach ven as the youngster's hand clawed at the butt of the gun. rank gave a croaking gasp and doubled over. His gun was ut but did him no good. Dusty's left fist came up, smashing to the youngster's jaw and lifting him erect, then the right ot across. The crack of the blow sounded loud, Frank olman's head snapped to one side, and he crashed down the ground.

Turning to Evans, Dusty was about to offer his apologies r the incident, but Frank Holman was not done. The oungster came to his hands and knees. He shook his head nd, through the roaring pain that fogged his brain, saw the olt lying on the ground. He dived forward, scooping the un up and rolling over to come to his knees with it in his and. Evans saw the move and yelled a warning, which rought Dusty spinning around. Dusty saw his danger and cted on it, his left hand leaping across his body to the hite-handled butt of the Colt in his right holster.

All his life Frank Holman had wanted to see a real fast an in action. Right in front of him was the fastest of them ll, but he never knew it. Half a second after Dusty's left and started to move, Frank Holman was dead.

The long-barreled army Colt came out and lined. There as no time to think of crippling Frank, sending a bullet rough his shoulder, not when he was lifting his gun, cocked and ready. Dusty shot for an instant kill, shot for the one place that would give him that result. The bullet smashed in, between Frank Holman's eyes, and shattered the back of his head as it came out. The youngster was almost lifted erect by the force of the heavy .44 ball. For an instant he was almost held erect, then he went down as if he'd been boned.

Dusty felt a push that sent him staggering, heard the crash of a shot and the slap of a bullet passing over his head going off into the darkness. Then he heard the dull boom of the Kid's old Dragoon and twisted to see what was happening.

The Ysabel Kid was watching the pale man by the Holman wagon. He saw the fast lift of the gun, lined shoulder high. It was a move that showed the man was more than just casually acquainted with handling guns. The Kid made his draw as he shoved Dusty, but even so he was almost too late.

Joubert saw this first shot miss and tried to correct his aim. He was in bad trouble and he knew it. There were two men, both ready to shoot, that he must deal with now. He took the Ysabel Kid as being the more dangerous of the two, bringing the old pinfire revolver into line and cocking it fast. He made a slight delay, but that delay was too long, far too long, when dealing with the Comanche-fast reactions of the Ysabel Kid. The old Dragoon gun bellowed out, kicked high as it vomited a round, soft lead ball from the seven-and-a-half-inch barrel. The .44 ball smashed into Joubert's body driving home into his chest.

Even so, had the Kid been armed with a lesser gun, he would have died. The Dragoon was loaded with a full forty grain charge, the heaviest load yet possible in any handgun. It hurled out a ball weighing a third of an ounce. A man hit by such a bullet did not remain on his feet; he was knocked down instantly.

This time was no exception. Joubert went over backward, his gun falling from his hand as he crashed to the ground.

At the sound of the shots men came running from all sides toward the Evans fire. They'd seen Frank Holman and the young Texan facing each other and, when Holman was nocked down, thought little of it, except that he'd got what e'd asked for. Now they crowded forward to see what was appening. They parted as Mrs. Holman ran from her 'agon, letting her through the crowd. With a shriek she ropped to her knees and lifted her son's bloody head and radled it. She made no other sound, and her eyes went to the big burly man who came running from the outer darkness. There was pain, grief, and a deep hatred as she looked t the man.

Major Brant arrived on the run. He could guess what had appened and snapped, "Tell it, Tracy."

"Young Holman here tried to force a fight on Dusty. You now how it was?" the scout replied, and there was a rumle of agreement from the crowd. "Dusty didn't want any rouble and tried to avoid it. Then Frank spat in his face and usty knocked him down. Turned his back on Frank, and he youngster picked his gun up to go for Dusty's back. usty turned and shot him, didn't have a choice."

"A likely story!" snarled the big man, forcing his way forard. "What chance would my boy have against a killer like 'usty Fog?"

"He didn't have a chance, Holman," Tracy replied evenly. Your boy never had a chance from the first day you let him rap on that gun. He thought he was fast, but he wasn't, ever would have been."

"You heard that!" Holman roared, swinging to face the orthern men in the crowd. "My boy was killed without a hance."

"Tracy never said anything like that!" Tapley Evans arked out. "Your boy came here looking for trouble, as he's ooked for it before. Only this time he got trouble and ouldn't handle it."

"Hear that!" yelled Holman. "Did you hear that? Them ebs are ganging up on us to protect that Texas killer."

"Hold it!" Brant snapped. "There's no cause to talk in that anner, Holman."

The *bête noire* of every wagon master taking a mixed rowd West was a revival of the old Civil War hatreds. Even fter eight years it was often absurdly easy to stir up trouble between the men of the North and the men of the South. So far Brant had never found himself with any such trouble but it looked as if it might boom open now.

"We ain't going to let them rebs get away with it, are we?" Holman yelled. "I got good cause to talk that way. Look how they've all ganged together, them rebs, to protect the man who killed my son. Are we going to let 'em get away with it?" He glared at the Northern men as he spoke, spitting out his hatred. "You, Caleb, you lost two sons fighting the rebs. Anse Keep, your brother died in Andersonville from the way they treated him. You, Ben, you lost a brother when Quantrell raided Lawrence. Are we going to—"

"Mister!" Dusty interrupted. "Did the man Lon here killed know you?"

"He was my friend. A sick man, a man who couldn't hardly see," Holman yelled back, shaking his fists wildly. His sleeves were rolled down, and there were wide leather cuffs protecting his wrists. "And that half-breed shot him."

"Easy, Lon," Dusty snapped, catching his friend's arm and holding him. He indicated the Northern men. "Send one of these gents to get the gun that man dropped, would you, Major?"

"Fetch it, please, Anse," Brant said to the tall, lean man who was the unspoken leader of the Northern men.

Anse Keep turned to fetch the revolver, and Dusty faced the crowd. "I came here looking for a man—"

"Hear that?" Holman bellowed. "Just hear that. He's admitting he came to kill poor old Hogan Joubert. You know he couldn't see without his glasses or with a gun."

The Northern men had to agree that they'd never seen Joubert without his glasses or with a gun. The thing was taking on a sinister note and getting worse all the time. The hotheads and the troublemakers, of whom there were always a few in any community, were getting ready to pitch in and start trouble. Brant would have a bad shooting scrape on his hands if he made a single move.

"Now, listen, all of you," he said, trying to calm things down. "I'll tell you why Captain Fog came here."

"We know why he came here!" Holman interrupted. "Us ankees are going to take him and hang him for murder."

Tapley Evans shook his head, hand hovering above the utt of his gun. "Not while any of us can pull a trigger."

That was all the waverers needed to make them throw .eir hands in with the side they supported in the war. The orthern men felt they must help one of their kind take the .urderer of his son. The Southern men were just as deter- .ined not to allow Captain Fog be taken by the Yankees.

"We licked them rebs once—" Holman began.

"Stop it! Stop it, all of you!" The woman they called rdma Brewster came from out of the darkness, her voice .ised and anger on her face. She stood between the two roups of men, right in the line of fire if shooting began. .ou take your hand from your gun, Tapley Evans. And you, .ll Woolsey. You stupid, hotheaded fools. Don't you realize .e've got miles ahead of us and our only hope of getting .rough those miles is to pull together?"

"Them rebs . . ." began a man, but his hand left his gun utt.

"Rebs?" The woman's tongue lashed him. "When your .orses need shoeing, you don't ask Tapley Evans who he .de for in the war. And when your wagons need new har- .ess, you go to Anse Keep. He doesn't ask if you wore blue . gray in the war. He goes right ahead and fixes it. When we .ad to help hand-haul wagons through that mud back in .ansas, we didn't think about the man who was helping us .ush wearing a different uniform in the war. We all pulled .d pushed together. We fought off that Indian attack the .me way. So stop your foolish talk of fighting and killing. .he South lost ninety thousand men before they called off .e fighting, but that did not make the hundred and ten .ousand and more Union men who died feel any better. .ver two hundred thousand men killed, countless more .rippled for life. Isn't that enough, or do you want more .lling now?"

Holman saw the other men wavering and turned his rage- .d hate-filled face at the woman. "You're a fine one to talk.

You lived in the South and sold them out. Her name's Eliz beth van Bruwer."

"The Yankee spy!" Tapley Evans growled out. "Is th true?"

"It is," replied the woman, meeting his eyes without w vering. "I'm Elizabeth van Bruwer, the Union spy. But I' also the woman who helped bring your son into the worl who treated and cared for Selina Brown and brought h through the fever. I tried to make up for what I did as m duty in the war—"

"Don't listen to the old hag," roared Holman, his ang making him slip up. "She was supposed to be working f the North but she sold me out to that damned Texan the after . . ." His voice trailed off, for he knew he'd said to much.

"I'd bet that leather cuff on your wrist covers an anch tattoo, mister." Dusty's voice cut through the silence th followed the man's words.

There was more than hate in Holman's face now; the was guilt and fear. He looked like a trapped animal, a r whose one way out of a pocket is to fight. It made him all th more dangerous.

"He's got one all right, Cap'n," Evans said. "I saw it o time when he was washing, only time I ever saw him wi them cuffs off."

"Come on, you Yankees!" Holman screamed, knowir some of the men might still follow him. "Let's take—"

"Not this time, Brace!"

The words brought Holman around to face the kneelir form of his wife. She was still nursing her son's head ar looking at her husband with a glint in her eyes he'd nev seen before. He clenched his right fist, the fist that had often beaten her into a bruised, sobbing heap.

"Shut your mouth!" he snarled.

"Not this time. I've held it shut for too long. Held it sh and took all your blows and abuse," she replied, spitting th words at him as if they were poison. "I've watched you ar that Hogan Joubert turn my son into a bully and troubl maker, teach him and make him think he was a good ma with a gun." Her eyes went to the crowd. "That young fella didn't kill my son. It was Brace Holman and Hogan Joubert who done it. They killed him the first day they gave him the gunbelt. You men, you think Holman was for you in the war. He wasn't—"

"Stop your mouth!" Holman roared, moving forward, foot drawing for a kick. Then he staggered back, face losing all its color.

Mrs. Holman was still kneeling, but she held her son's army Colt, gripped it in both her hands, lining it. The hammer was drawn back, and Holman knew how light the trigger was set. It would take only the gentlest pull to allow the hammer to fall, and at that range she could not miss.

Holman fell back a step or two; the look in his wife's eyes scared him. He opened his mouth to say something.

"You'll do nothing to me," she hissed, the long years of cruelty and abuse boiling up inside her. "Not now or at all. Not when those folks know how you sold arms to the South in the war. You tried to get Grandma Brewster there killed by a lynch mob when you heard the war was over. The Pinkertons were looking for you, and she knew about that anchor on your wrist, so you had to get rid of her. You went to her hometown, you and that Joubert, who was supposed to be half-blind and not able to use a gun. I've seen him use one, and kill men from behind with it."

"Don't listen to her." Holman gasped, for he could see the men of the crowd were wavering and believing. He saw Anse Keep looking down at Joubert's body, after finding the gun that Joubert's last convulsions had flung under the wagon. The man held the revolver and was looking down, with the aid of a lantern, for something more. "She's tetched in the head."

"I'm not. Though I should be with the way you've treated me all these years. You folks look under the floorboards of our wagon. There's rifles—"

With a beastlike snarl Holman leapt forward, lifting his hands to smash down his wife and silence her tongue. There was a crash, and smoke curled from the gun in the woman's hands. Holman stiffened up as the lead drove upward into his body. He stood for a moment, hands clawing down at the hole the bullet made, then he pitched forward onto his face. Mrs. Holman stared with unseeing eyes at the big shape, then dropped the gun and collapsed across the body of her son.

Brant looked around, his face pale. "Get the doctor here."

By now the women of the train were forming up in one body, but the men were still in two separate groups, the old hatreds of the war not settled down yet. All looked at the others and waited for someone to make the first move. It was still a dangerous situation and could rip the train wide open at the seams if handled wrong.

"Look at you," Elizabeth van Bruwer snapped, still between the men. "Grown men. Responsible men. Men with families. You're acting like children. Do you think you can get to your new homes without each other? You Union men think Major Brant will go with you because he rode for the Union. But how far will you get without a scout? That's right, Tracy Wade rode for the South, in Mosby's Rangers. How far will you Union men get without a blacksmith? Will you Confederates be able to repair your own leatherwork? Think on it before you split up. I recognized Holman soon after we left the East, but I never said anything. I thought he was going to make a new life in the West, so I let him be. The war is over; it ended for you at the Appomattox Courthouse, but it never ended for me, not until I joined this train. For eight years I never spoke to a living soul other than my two servants. They had to buy my food in the Negro market because no one would serve the Union spy. I did not hate them for it. They were my friends and I betrayed them. A mob was going to lynch me and Captain Fog there stopped them. I thought out who the man you sent your friends to look for might have been later, Captain. I also thought long on what you told me, about having to face the peace."

"Why're you going West, ma'am?" asked Dusty, watching Keep coming back with the revolver.

"My kin all went North when the war started, but I stayed behind to do what I could for my country and my beliefs. After the war, up North I was an asset to them. I was Elizaeth van Bruwer, the Union spy, someone who brought redit to the family. Then they came South to go into politics, and I was no longer an asset; I was something to be hidden. It would do a bright young politician no good to have a Union spy for kin. So I was put on this train, sent West for my health. The folks thought my name was Brewster and called me Grandma. I didn't argue with them. It was so good to be accepted, to have people speak to me, that I did not mention my real name. Well, you know who I am now."

There was silence, uneasy silence now. Anse Keep was trying to get through the crowd with the revolver and the news of what he'd seen, or failed to see, in the Holman wagon.

Mrs. Evans moved forward, passing her husband to stand by Elizabeth van Bruwer and look at the crowd. Her Southern drawl was gentle and not loud, yet it carried clear around the circle.

"Mrs. Keep, I think the ladies' sewing circle meets at your wagon tonight. Grandma Brewster will preside at it as usual."

There was a low murmur of approval from the other Southern women, and Anse Keep's wife moved forward to side with Mrs. Evans, her New England accent backing up the Southern woman's words.

"Anse Keep, finish your business, then don't stop too late playing poker with Tapley Evans. But don't come to our wagon unless you've been playing."

The tension left the air. The men could see that their women were as one in the determination not to allow Civil War hatreds to break up the train. Tapley Evans stepped to Elizabeth van Bruwer and touched his hat brim.

"Ma'am, the war ended in '65. We can't undo all the years down South, but we'll try."

Anse Keep came through the crowd and went to Brant, holding out the revolver. "That's it, Major. Never saw one like it before. But for a man who was half-blind, he could sure shoot without his spectacles."

"Did you see what color his eyes were, mister?" asked Dusty.

"Couldn't see all that well, but they looked to be light blue, pale eyes," Keep replied and looked at the letter Dusty held toward him. "What's that?"

"The description of a man who killed five Texans in the Fair Lady saloon in Mulrooney. A man who used a ten-shot pinfire revolver."

Anse Keep read the letter and the description. He nodded his head and passed it to Tapley Evans.

"I think you got your man, Captain Fog."

The following morning Dusty was by the side of "Grandma Brewster's" wagon. He had just come from watching the floorboards of the Holman wagon torn up and a hundred Winchesters with ammunition for them brought to light. He climbed into the van Bruwer wagon and looked at the scared, pallid face of Mrs. Holman, who lay in the bed.

"Are you going to take me back?" she asked weakly.

Dusty smiled. "Why'd I do a fool thing like that, ma'am? You aim to go to California, not back to Kansas."

"You work for a sheriff, don't you?"

"Only for one thing, ma'am. And I've done that. Can you tell me for sure if Joubert went into Mulrooney that night you were camped nearby?"

"Yes," she agreed, looking at Major Brant and Elizabeth van Bruwer, who were now in the wagon. "He went on in and got into bad trouble. He told Hogan about it, been a bad shooting. You going to try me for murder, Major?"

"No, ma'am. There'll be a coroner's jury, but it'll be brought as self-defense. Help Captain Fog all you can."

"Joubert run into a man who used to work with them when they were running arms to the South in the war. They went to some saloon to kill a bunch of Texans. Joubert was scared that somebody'd come after him."

"How about those rifles, ma'am?" Dusty asked.

"We fixed to leave the train and sell them to a half-breed. This's the sixth trip we've made. Hogan fixed to leave the train in a couple of days and meet up with the renegade. Now I don't know what I'll do."

Elizabeth van Bruwer smiled gently. "That'll be all for now, Captain."

Dusty was satisfied. He would take an affidavit, signed by Major Brant and other men in the train, to the effect that the men who had killed the five Texans were dead. Clay Allison would be satisfied by that; there would be no trouble in Mulrooney.

Standing by his big paint stallion, Dusty looked at Elizabeth van Bruwer and thought of the other time they had met. To his rear the Kid sat his big white stallion ready to head back to Mulrooney and their friends.

"Well, Captain," she said, smiling at him. "We're going our separate ways, and I doubt if we'll meet again. It's strange, but both our meetings have involved the same man."

"Yes, ma'am," Dusty agreed, mounting his horse and touching his hat to her. "I read something somewhere, I don't remember where. The mills of the gods grind slow, but they grind exceedingly small."

Elizabeth van Bruwer watched Dusty Fog and the Ysabel Kid riding up the slope. They headed back to Mulrooney, then home to Texas. A small man riding by the side of a tall man. But she'd never think of Dusty Fog as small.

PART THREE
THE PAINT

The horse stood alone in the breaking pen, smallest of the three pole-walled corrals before the OD Connected ranch house. It was a magnificent horse, seventeen hand of uncut, uncurried, savage beauty with the small, shapely head and graceful, proudly arched neck of a Thoroughbred. Its mane and tail were long and flowing, the mane snow-white, the tail a deep, rich deer-red. The powerful quarters, firm, straight back, and the great barrel of body told of stamina, power, and strength. Yet for all of that there was no hint of cloddiness or slowness about the horse, nor was there any sign of spindly long-legged growth. The horse was perfectly proportioned for its great size. In color it was white, with splashes of deep deer-red, a paint and a beauty in any man's book. Standing alone and proud, it seemed to tower over the horses in the next corral like a giant among pygmies.

The paint caught Old Devil Hardin's eye as he came from the porch of the OD Connected house and walked down to the corrals with Dusty Fog and Red Blaze at his sides. It took his full attention for all of a minute, before he even looked at the other horses that awaited his expert inspection.

The war was long over, and Ole Devil was back in the Rio Hondo country, preparing to get the OD Connected ranch on its feet after years of fighting and neglect. Before anything could be done, the great roundup he and Dusty planned, or any of the other numerous tasks started, the remuda must be rebuilt and given fresh blood.

So word went to a horse trader to bring along the best he could manage, and he came fast, ready to greet his oldest and favorite customer. His speed in coming, with the best he had to offer, was not only due to his desire to sample some of Ole Devil's good gold, it was a genuine friendship. Ole Devil was buying, and that was all Trader Schell needed to know. Ole Devil asked for the best, be it stud horse, brood mare, or plain remuda gelding.

A ranch could be made or broken by its remuda, the band of saddle horses that supplied mounts for the cowhands of the spread. Ole Devil ran a remuda of well over a hundred horses and, before the war, every one was potentially a good cow horse. Every one must also be a gelding, that was a firm rule of any remuda, and for good reason. Mares were not used in the remuda, since they were likely to become bunch quitters, pulling out of the remuda and heading for home. The trouble then was that no self-respecting he-horse would think of letting a lady go home unescorted, and the remuda found itself shy, not only of the mare but of several horses. Stallions were not used due to their habit of fighting and otherwise stirring up a peaceable remuda.

A horse was put into the remuda when it was around four years old. Two years later it could be considered a trained cow horse, but did not really reach its full value until it was ten years old. Under normal conditions the remuda would be culled out before each spring roundup; the old horses, or those proved to be unsuitable for one reason or another, would be taken out and either turned loose to graze or sold off.

The three men who ran the OD Connected ranch went to the second of the large corrals and looked at the bunch of horses that milled around in it. Red Blaze's elder, twin brothers ran a ranch that bordered the OD Connected, but he preferred to stay and work with his cousin Dusty and be at the center of things in the great Hardin, Blaze, and Fog cattle empires. Dusty was ranch *segundo,* second-in-command to Ole Devil, and was tipped as being the one who would succeed Ole Devil to leadership of the clan.

Trader Schell watched the three men approaching with a delighted grin on his face. He was a plump, yet somehow rubbery-looking man in working clothes. He did not look to be, but was, one of the finest horse busters in Texas. His one

nterest in life was horses, catching them, busting them, and
rading them off. It was said he'd rather not sell a horse than
et it go without a long dicker over the price. Today he
vould need his top skill, for he was up against a master at
he horse-trading game. Even though both he and Ole Devil
new the price that would be paid, in fact the money was
ving ready in Ole Devil's gun-decorated study; they would
ave a long haggle before the price was reached. Trader
chell's visits to the OD Connected were the high spots of
is life, he looked forward to them the way a child looked
orward to a pleasant holiday.

"How'd they look to you, Devil?" he asked.

It was like the start of an often-seen but well-liked play.
chell, Hardin, Dusty, Red, and the assembled OD Con-
ected hands could have said the words and given the an-
wer from long experience.

"Fair, not better'n fair. When you fixing in to bring me
ome decent stock in?"

Ole Devil liked the look of the horses and knew he'd have
een hard pushed to find better, but he wouldn't think of
etting Schell know. That would spoil all the anticipated fun.
his was to be a battle between two master traders, even
hough the prices were a foregone conclusion.

Being the buyer it was up to Ole Devil to make the first
nove. His play was to act as if he'd never seen such poor
torses, that he couldn't care whether he bought such a poor
ot or not. He snorted, his facial expression showing the
isgust he felt at the offering in the corral.

"Where the hell did you pick 'em up from? Some mange-
overed Digger Indian?"

Schell's own facial expression was something to see. A
nixture of annoyance and exasperation at the slander on
is stock, pride in his horses, and complete indifference to
elling the bunch to Ole Devil. He started to extol the many
nd varied virtues of the horses, spreading on every empha-
is he could think to their superb breeding and capabilities.
o hear him, it would appear he was doing Ole Devil a great
avor in offering the horses for sale at all.

All in all it was a masterly display and one that could have made many a professional actor jealous. The hands of the ranch were all gathered listening, grinning, and nudging each other at every move in the lightning-fast cut-and-thrust of the trading match.

Dusty was only half listening, storing up pointers for the future. His main attention was on the horses as they circled and milled in the corral. In his capacity as ranch *segundo* Dusty would have much to do with the remuda, almost more than Ole Devil himself. He'd looked the big paint over and so far it did not come into his calculations at all. It was a fine horse, would make a good stud, but it was a stallion and would never run in the remuda.

So Dusty's horse-wise eyes studied the horses, picking the rough mounts in his mind. They were the horses that would take the most handling and would form his personal mount; the Texan never used the term *string* for the horses assigned to him for his work on the ranch. It was a mount and could run from three, on a small ranch, to a dozen, on a spread the size of the OD Connected.

A hand selected the horses for his mount in a choosing match and was bound by his pick. Not even the boss could interfere with a man's selection of his mount. If he cared for the horses, the man was left with them; if he did not, he would soon know about it, and if the boss changed a horse in a man's mount, it was taken as a hint that his services were no longer wanted.

Dusty would take the rough string, the fighters, and the horses with a good big bellyfull of bedsprings. He took them because he was the *segundo* of the ranch and would never ask a man to ride a horse he could not sit astride.

Schell decided on a change of tactics and set up a crafty distraction, which was one of the reasons he brought the paint along.

"Now, there's a hoss for you, Devil," he announced modestly, waving a hand to break the pen. "Just about the finest stud I ever come across. Run faster'n a Neuces steer, swim better'n a black bass, and jump higher 'n' further than a cougar. Now, I ain't the one to boast—"

"Never yet saw a paint as was worth sic 'em as a workin'

hoss," replied Ole Devil, eyeing the big horse with a disdain he was far from feeling. "They always work slow, never learn how to cut and handle cattle, and they fight the bit."

"Not this'n," protested Schell, and launched into a vivid description of the paint's good points.

"Color don't count if the colt can't trot," growled Ole Devil, using an old range saying. "That paint looks a mite spavined to me."

Schell raised his eyes to heaven as if seeking strength to defend himself against such a libelous attack on his horse. Then, as if despairing of talking any sense to Ole Devil, he turned to Dusty.

"What do you reckon to the paint, Cap'n?"

"Too big for a cow hoss," replied Dusty, no mean hand at the trading game himself. "Tell you, though, I'll give you a Yankee general's dress sword for it and chance being robbed."

"I wouldn't even take it as boot for the deal," grunted Schell. Boot was some article thrown in over and above the final reached price in a trading deal and went to the winner of the deal. "How about you, Red?"

"I'll give you all of five dollars and a Spencer carbine with a bust magazine spring for it," answered Red. "Then I'd be overpaying you. I suppose the paint'd be all right for riding into town on."

Schell grinned, and winked at Ole Devil. Young Red's voice sounded just right, like a man who finally, after much thought, found something the big paint would be useful at. The two boys were learning real well, considering they'd been fighting Yankees for most of their growing years. Give them a few more years of watching Ole Devil in action and they'd be all set to trade with the best in the land. Schell chuckled and, feeling refreshed with the change of topic, turned his attention back to the remuda horses.

Dusty watched the battle begin once more and caught Ole Devil's nod. He knew full well what the nod meant and, ignoring Ole Devil's bellow that such a mangy wind-broke bunch of crow bait was no use to him, turned toward the corral. He watched the horses milling for a moment, then turned to the watching hands.

"Kiowa, snake out that line back and let's take a good look at it," he said, jerking his thumb toward a dun gelding with a black stripe running the length of its back. Then he looked at Billy Jack, who lounged by the corral side, rope in hand. "Happen you can land him, Billy Jack, I'd take it kind if you'd bring that Appaloosa in."

Billy Jack's miserable expression intensified at having work thrust onto him. He swung up onto the rail and watched the horses moving by him. Despite his appearance, Billy Jack was a roper second to none. He could make that sixty-foot length of three-strand, hard-plaited manila rope come alive in his hands. Men who'd seen Billy Jack perform with a rope swore the only thing he couldn't do with it was make it stand straight up in the air, climb up it, and vanish from the top.

The horse Dusty called for came around in the milling group. It was a big, washy bay horse; the color fading to almost white at the rump, which was splashed with black spots; it showed a lack of hair on the inside of the thighs and in the tail; the nose was pinkish; and there was a lot of white in the eye. The horse was an Appaloosa, a type bred and raised by the Nez Percé Indians. They were a northern tribe that never came into Texas, so Dusty wondered how such a horse came to be in the bunch. He would never have thought of asking.

Billy Jack watched the horse, measuring the distance with his eye. Then the rope came alive in his hands, making one fast whirl up to the right, over his head, and sailed out in a well-timed, accurate hooley-ann throw. It was a roper's throw much used for taking horses from a milling bunch, made with the minimum of fuss. A small-loop head catch enabled several men to take horses at the same time. The loop flew true, and Billy Jack watched the *honda* sliding, tightening the circle as it flew. His talented wrists caused the rope to turn and flatten out above the Appaloosa's head, then drop gently over it. Billy Jack twitched the rope and tightened the noose until there was no chance of the horse slipping it again. With his horse caught, Billy Jack slid down from the rail and led it through the partly opened gate.

Dusty and Red went to the two horses and examined them thoroughly, checked eyes, teeth, condition of coat, hooves, and made sure everything was all right. There was no fooling about or slacking in the work, and both the young men knew what they were doing. Finally Dusty looked at the horses' holders.

"Trot them up and down a piece for me."

Billy Jack groaned at the order, even though he had known it would come. He was a cowhand, regarding any work that could not be done from the back of a horse as being fit only for farmers or Yankees.

"You mean on foot?" he asked. "Walking?"

"Nope. Running!"

The horses were moved up and down before Dusty, allowing him to see them in their various paces, making sure there was nothing wrong with them. He doubted if anything would be wrong. Trader Schell would bring only the best to the OD Connected. The check was a matter of form. Ole Devil expected it; so did Schell.

When the horses stopped, Dusty walked in front of the Appaloosa again and stood rubbing his jaw, giving Billy Jack a few anxious moments. The miserable one knew Dusty's sense of humor might call for another session of trotting, a thing that would do Billy Jack's already aching feet no good at all. With this in mind Billy Jack gave out a warning.

"Never look a gift horse in the mouth."

"Why, sure," agreed Dusty. "But we're buying this lot, don't forget. They're not gifts, so it doesn't count." He watched the anxious expression on Billy Jack's face for a moment, then grinned. "They'll do. Put them in the other corral. Lane, bring in that dun. Tex, I'll have that bay coyote here."

Billy Jack and Kiowa led off the two horses, turning them into the empty third corral, and Dusty went to look over the next pair of horses. Dusty went on with his work, ignoring the bellow from Ole Devil that we wouldn't buy such a useless bunch of trash and Trader Schell's assertion that he was damned if he wouldn't take the next lot of horses and sell them to the Yankee cavalry, where they'd be appreciated.

Horse after horse was caught and brought for Dusty's inspection. He and Red worked fast, but they worked with care. Any inattention to his work might mean Dusty missed something and would bring down a bitter rebuke on his head, the more bitter because it would make Ole Devil break off his dickering. Dusty knew that even while arguing at full pitch, Ole Devil was watching the horses with care and missing nothing.

Of all the horses only one was not suitable and Schell had given his men orders to leave it, but somehow it became mixed in with the others. He was annoyed, but knew Ole Devil accepted his apology.

The price was finally agreed upon as the last of the horses were checked. Ole Devil snorted and swore he'd bring his next bunch in from a Yankee dealer, and Schell growled back that the loss he'd taken on the sale would put him out of business so it wouldn't bother him. The price was what they both knew from the start it would be, although Schell held out for the Yankee general's dress sword and the Springfield carbine with the bust magazine springs as boot.

Dusty gave orders for the branding of the horses to begin then turned to Schell.

"Have they been three-saddled yet, Trader?" he asked.

"All of them," was the reply. "All bar the paint."

"Why not him?" inquired Old Devil.

"Because I'm a red-blooded Texas coward and I aims to keep all my blood inside where it belongs, not outside where it shows. I'm sorta modest like that. It took us near on all one day to get shoes on that hoss."

The words gave Dusty and Ole Devil a warning of what to expect from the big paint stallion. Trader Schell and his men made their living riding and busting bad horses. It took one out of the ordinary to worry them. They'd three-saddled the rest of the animals, ridden each horse the three times that any bronc buster would before claiming it was gentle enough to be handed on to the cowhand, but they left the big paint alone. Despite Schell's words Ole Devil and Dusty knew a try had been made to ride the big horse. If Schell's men could not handle the horse, it would take a good man to stay afork it.

The paint was a challenge and Ole Devil was never the man to resist a challenge. The big horse would make a fine stud, even with the rangeland prejudice against paints as working mounts. So he meant to have the paint, although he was going to make a good haggle over the price.

When the deal was concluded, even as the branding fires were lit and the OD Connected irons heated, Ole Devil invited Schell to finish the deal on the porch. Calling Dusty along, the owner of the ranch led the way to the cool shade of the porch. A pair of big redbone hounds lay sprawled out in the shade, pounding their tails in welcome but making no effort to move as the men came up. Dusty grinned, and gently stirred the bitch with his toe. She beat her tail harder but made no move to get up, so he stepped over her and took a chair.

Tommy Okasi, Ole Devil's Japanese servant, materialized from inside the house with a tray bearing glasses, a bottle of Burgundy, and a bottle of beer. He handed out the drinks and withdrew again. Dusty poured out his beer and sat back in his chair.

"Fair bunch of hosses, Trader."

"Good as I could raise. The Ronde River bottoms are swarming with wild hosses just waiting to be brought in. There's a helluva lot of buffalo wolves up there. I made a fair price on wolf skins from my last trip. Aim to go up that way again as soon as the boys have spent their pay and are ready for work."

"Got us some old cock turkeys in the Rio Hondo brakes that are bigger than buffalo wolves," remarked Ole Devil. "Doc Gorman and Hondo aim to come out at the end of the week and take us on a hunting trip. You feel like staying on?"

"Nope, I'll come back on Saturday and move out with you if I've done my business. Want to sell off the culls from your bunch to the Yankee cavalry."

Billy Jack slouched up at that moment, his face smudged with grime from the branding fire. He jerked a thumb toward the Polveroso trail and said, "We got some callers, Devil."

Three men were riding toward the house, coming along the trail from the county seat. Trader Schell studied them and gave an angry snort as if he recognized them, although he did not offer to say whether he did or not.

The three men rode good horses, but none of them looked like cowhands and one definitely was not. He rode slightly ahead of the other two, clearly leading them, not riding as a friend. He wore a high-crowned, snow-white hat of a style rarely seen in Texas. His hair hung shoulder long and was combed, showing considerable attention had been taken with it. His face was tanned, his mustache big and flowing, his short, pointed beard showing the same care as did his hair. His eyes were hard and spoiled a handsome face; the hardness of them was one of cruelty. It gave him the look of a man who would get his own way or pull every dirty trick until he did. His clothes caught the eye, the long-fringed, bead-decorated buckskin jacket, the snow-white shirt and the black bow tie were not the dress of a working cowhand, nor were the skintight trousers placed carefully into the top of his shining boots. Around his waist was a fancy-looking gunbelt, and a pearl-handled army Colt rested in the Missouri holster, the whole of the trigger guard exposed to the view. He rode a fine-looking, yet nervous sorrel horse, his saddle a silver-decorated rig that had cost plenty, and from under his leg rose the butt of a Henry rifle, the barrel nickel plated instead of being blue.

There was something about the man that Dusty took a dislike to right away. It was partly the dandy dress, partly the arrogant way the man looked around him. Mostly it was because of the horse. That man would never break a horse with kindness; he would always use the cruelest method he could find. The ghost cord and the long-lashed whip would be his way.

The other two were good on their horses, but they were not cowhands. Dusty could read the signs; he knew cowhands, and those two had never worked for any brand. Their clothes were a hybrid mixture of army and civilian such as many men wore with the war so recently over. Both wore low-tied guns and looked to be hard citizens, but that did not worry Dusty Fog. He was by way of being a hard citizen himself when there was need for it.

Passing the branding fires and the scene of cowland industry, they brought the horses to a halt in front of the ranch house. The fancy-dressed leader of the trio glanced at the breaking pen and the big paint stallion that stood in it, then turned his eyes to the men on the porch. His voice was loud, bombastic, and arrogant as he spoke:

"See, the paint's still about, Trader. How much do you want for him?"

Trader Schell frowned at this breach of hospitality. The man had no right to come discussing business with him on Ole Devil's property. There was no friendship in his voice as he replied:

"You're too late, Covacs. I've sold him to Ole Devil here."

"That so?" the man called Covacs asked, turning his eyes to Ole Devil. "I'll give you fifty dollars on top of whatever you paid for the paint."

"He's not for sale," growled Ole Devil, annoyed at the breach of etiquette. The man should have waited to be asked to dismount before trying to do business. He was too hospitable to hold back the next words. "Light and rest your saddles."

Dusty watched the three men and wished he was wearing his guns. He rarely, if ever, wore his gunbelt when working around the ranch house, and none of the crew were armed, although Schell was still wearing his gun.

"All right," Covacs grunted. "I'll make it seventy-five on top of whatever you paid for it. In gold."

"I said he's not for sale," replied Ole Devil in a tone that indicated the matter was closed.

"Look, General," Covacs went on, seeing the ranch hands watching him. He knew whose ranch this was and knew that behind him was probably as tough a ranch crew as a man could find in the West. There was no chance of rough stuff to get the horse. "I run a traveling show. You may have heard of it, Colonel Blade Covacs' Circus Giganticus. I want that paint to bill him as the horse that nobody can ride."

"And I want the horse myself."

There was nothing Covacs could do in the face of such an answer. His eyes went to the breaking pen, feasting on the huge paint stallion. There was a horse in a thousand. Such an eye-catching horse, suitably treated, could be turned into a vicious and most unmanageable killer, a horse that no living man would be able to ride. The paint showed every sign of being able to uphold such a title; it had the size and strength without being slow, awkward, or passive.

There was no way of getting the paint legally, for Ole Devil owned it and would have his brand burned on its flank soon, showing to the world who owned it. There was no taking the horse by force either. Three men could not hold down the OD Connected ranch crew, and horse stealing was a hanging offense anywhere west of the Big Muddy. Covacs knew this and he gave way on it.

"All right, it's a pity," he said, a shifty gleam in his eyes. "Do you have any more horses to sell, Trader?"

"Nope!" replied Schell, making it plain in that one word that even if he did, he would not sell any to Covacs. "I just sold Ole Devil all I've got to spare and won't have any more until I go out again."

"Up to the Ronde River country where you got the paint?" inquired Covacs, resentment and annoyance showing plain in his tones as he mentioned the big horse.

Trader Schell was noncommittal. "Might be, might not."

"I may see you up there," grunted Covacs, and turned to leave.

"Water your hosses and go up to the cookshack for a meal, if you like," Ole Devil growled. "Billy Jack, come and show these *hombres* the cookshack."

Covacs nodded, although he gave the impression that he thought he should be invited onto the porch for a drink and his food. He could see that no such invitation was likely to be forthcoming, so he went with his men.

"Man'd say you don't like that *hombre*, Trader," Dusty remarked as the three men followed Billy Jack toward the cookshack.

"I can't say I do, although he never done me no hurt. He was up in the Ronde River bottoms while I was rounding up those hosses. Was hunting for wild hosses himself, but he didn't know much about it. Got set on that paint stallion and was a mote riled when I caught it. Thought we'd have some trouble with him, but my boys outnumbered his. I left one day while he was out after a bunch of broomtails. He's a bad, mean cuss with a hoss and I didn't want him to have his hands on the paint."

"What's he do for a living?" Dusty asked.

"Like he says, runs a tent show. Ran it all through the war, and I don't know where he got to be a colonel. His show's as crooked as they come, from all I heard. I reckon he wanted the paint to do just what he said."

Ole Devil's eyes went to the paint. It was a fine horse, too good to be turned into a vicious killer to enrich the owner of a tent show. Ole Devil was a hard and stern man, but he was never cruel and would never allow any cruelty in breaking a horse of his brand. His men all respected him for it; they knew his remuda was good and aimed to keep it that way. The paint would never be a remuda horse, but at least at the OD Connected it would lead a useful life and not be turned into a vicious killer hating all men.

The three men rode off soon after, followed from a distance by Billy Jack, Kiowa, and another hand, who were on Dusty's orders to see Covacs and his party well out of the OD Connected house's immediate range. Dusty was a suspicious young man and did not trust Covacs, having seen the way the man looked at the big paint.

Covacs knew of the escort and ignored it. For one thing he did not plan any move to get hold of the paint—yet. The other reason was that the three Texans were all armed. Covacs was no fool. The laws of the West were hard, direct, and very sensible in dealing with horse thieves. There was no pleading first offense and receiving a small sentence. A horse thief was hung on the spot, if he wasn't shot, for in a country where to be without a horse was to be in danger of death, horse stealing was classed as murder and treated accordingly.

So Covacs rode on. His tent show was some forty miles to the West, well over the Rio Hondo county line. Hondo Fog, sheriff of Rio Hondo County, would never stand for the crooked play of the tent show, and Covacs did not believe in taking chances, not when there were other towns not so well policed waiting to be fleeced.

"Are they still after us?" he asked.

"Yeah," grunted one of his men. "Naw, they ain't. They stopped up on that rim back there. Be able to watch us for miles."

"Let 'em," Covacs replied. "The fresh air'll do them good. They'll go back and tell Hardin we've gone. We'll leave a couple of weeks so they forget, then one night come back. One way or another I'm going to have that paint."

Back at the ranch the branding went on fast. The men were all experts, and the horses passed through their hands in rapid succession. Each horse was caught, thrown carefully to avoid hurting it, then the glowing, red-hot brand was applied to the rump, leaving the mark by which all men knew Ole Devil Hardin's cattle and horses, OD Connected. The two letters O and D, the side of the O touching the straight bar of the D.

It was an exciting business, for the horses were anything but friendly when they got to their feet, and several of the hands had narrow escapes. The big paint gave most trouble of all, but finally that, too, was branded. It would have been a brave man who would have gone into the breaking pen to the horse when it was released. The paint stood snorting, clearly promising the first man who did come in that he ould not walk out again. Ole Devil watched the horse, nowing it was as good as he'd ever owned. The big paint as going to make a first-class stud and a fine go-to-town orse, a fine and eye-catching mount for him—if he could de it.

The following morning Ole Devil ate a light breakfast and eft the house. His coat and hat lay on the porch, his trousers were tucked into sharp-toed, high-heeled cowboy oots. From his wrist hung a quirt, a foot-long, woven-eather whip, the short handle weighted with lead. This was ot to beat the horse with but to knock it back to its feet if it eared up and looked like it would fall over backward.

The first thing Ole Devil saw was that the men were sadling the horse in the bronc stall that was attached to, and pened into, the breaking pen. The bronc staff was a narrow nclosure, just wide enough to allow the horse to enter and ave a saddle slipped on. It was something the cowhands arely used, only the most dangerous of horses being acorded such treatment. That Dusty was using it for the big aint warned Ole Devil of the stormy times ahead.

Dusty waited until Red fixed the blindfold over the paint's yes, then made a final check that the saddle was firmly irthed home. He led the big paint out and knew that the orse was only waiting, not accepting the fact of being sadled as a sign of man's mastery. That Trader Schell's men ad roped and saddle-broken the horse was plain to Dusty. did not fight a mounted man's rope and accepted the addle, taking both calmly as if saving up every ounce of trength and energy to deal with any man fool enough to try o sit that saddle.

Ole Devil went forward, ducking between the thick pole ails of the breaking pen and walking toward the horse. The reaking pen was the smallest of the three corrals, the one here bad horses were ridden, horses that could not be andled on the open range. In the center of the pen a tenoot-long, strong post was buried half its length and firmly acked home in the soil. This was the snubbing post; a bad orse could be snubbed down to the post when necessary nd tied firmly to allow safe handling. With a normally bad horse the snubbing post would have been used for the saddling, but not with the big paint.

"Let me take him, Uncle Devil," Dusty suggested eagerly longing for the chance to ride the big horse.

Ole Devil shook his head, smiling grimly. He could not allow any man, even his *segundo*, to ride the big paint until he made a try at it. That was Ole Devil's firm rule, never to ask a man to do anything Ole Devil could not do himself. He went to the paint and nodded to Red, who ducked out of the corral. Only Dusty was left inside with Ole Devil and the horse, for when the rancher mounted, there would be all hell uncorked, and the fewer men to duck out of the corral the safer it would be. Dusty stood holding the horse's head while Ole Devil checked the double girths and made sure everything in the saddle and bridle were set safe. There was no implied censure of Dusty's work in the move. It was one that Dusty and all the watching men approved of, one they would have taken had they been in Ole Devil's shoes.

"Want me to take the bedsprings out'n him first, Devil?" called Billy Jack.

There was a laugh at the words, Billy Jack's offer to ride the fight out of the paint before Ole Devil mounted. Then silence fell as Ole Devil gripped the saddle horn and swung up, throwing his leg over, finding the stirrup iron, and setting his foot firmly in it.

Dusty held the horse, watching his uncle for the sign to pull off the blindfold, then get out of the corral—fast. He could see the paint's muscles bunching as the big horse prepared to show this impertinent man creature who was boss.

Ole Devil settled himself, gave Dusty a nod, and prepared for action. Dusty pulled the blindfold and flung himself to one side, diving through the corral rails and coming to his feet.

The big paint stood for an instant as if planning its campaign. Then it went into its fight. It left the ground in a long jump, going high into the air, then, as it started to come down, kicked its hindquarters high again. The moment all

ur feet touched the ground the horse hurled up some
ore, with another long, high, rump kicking bound.

"A straight bucker," Red grunted as other hands yelled
eir approval.

Dusty nodded in agreement. A straight bucker fought in
e way and only one way. With long, high jumps, without
y rearing, twisting, and turning for variety. It was the tac-
: of a big and powerful horse, very rough in action, for the
rse went high, then, as it started to come down, sent its
mp up again. The straight-bucking horse was either easy
handle or hard and dangerous. The paint was not one of
e easy kind. One thing was for sure. The man who came
a straight bucker almost always got hurt, for the horse
rew him high and hard.

Ole Devil took five of the high, rump-kicking jumps,
eased the horse was fighting sensibly and was not a blind
cker, hurling itself wildly without watching where it was
ing.

Then the horse brought off its sixth jump, going even
gher and making a more savage rump kick at the end of it.
e Devil felt his seat leave the saddle as the horse started
drop under him and he was aware of what would come
xt. He tried to kick his feet free of the stirrups, but the
ght foot jammed for a vital instant. The cantle of the sad-
e, driven up by the high-flung hindquarters, smashed into
e Devil's seat, sending numbing agony driving through
m and almost knocking him unconscious. Then he was
rown high and smashed down on his back, the force of the
nding driving the breath from his body. A dull, numbing,
w, aching pain filled Ole Devil. Through it he heard the
lls of the men and the thunder of hooves as the big paint
nt on, still throwing the straight bucks, not realizing the
ler was gone. The yells and the sound of hooves were
owing fainter as Ole Devil felt the pain welling away. He
t sleepy, and the sight of the huge horse rearing high over
m, slashing iron-shod hooves, appeared half real and
urred.

Dusty saw what was happening and realized the danger
instant before any of the others. He snatched the rope

from Billy Jack's hand, ducking between the rails and racin
forward. The big paint ran on for a couple of leaps afte
throwing Ole Devil, and that was what saved the rancher
life.

Disregarding his danger, Dusty darted forward. He was o
foot and knew the big horse would come for him as soon a
it felt the touch of the rope. That did not stop Dusty for a
instant. His uncle was down and the horse would come bac
to stomp Ole Devil to a pulp unless there was a distractior
Dusty built the loop as he ran; he would make the distra-
tion or die trying.

The rope sailed out, flying loop hurling up toward th
paint's head as it reared above Ole Devil. Dusty braced him
self on his high heels and, as the loop fell over the horse
head, pulled backward with all his strength. His weight an
the leverage of the rope brought the horse down onto i
four feet, the front hooves smashing into the ground scar
inches from Ole Devil's head.

Landing on its feet, the big paint let out a scream of rag
and came charging at Dusty. He turned and ran for it, hea
ing the thunder of hooves as the paint came after him. Th
snubbing post was ahead, and Dusty skimmed it, throwin
out his free arm to hook it around it and swing himself in
tight circle. The horse could not turn quickly enough an
went by. Dusty threw a loop of rope around the post an
took up slack as the paint charged again. It was still a da
gerous business, trying to avoid the horse and handle th
rope.

Red Blaze raced to where a horse stood saddled an
ready for the hands going out to work on the range. He wer
into the saddle with a flying bound, tearing the reins fre
and bringing the horse in a tight turn, then hurling it for th
corral. He was only a hair's breadth ahead of Kiowa, an
they raced their horses forward to where Billy Jack wa
throwing the poles of the gate to one side. The two me
rode forward, ropes in their hands, converging on the pair
The loops flew out and the big horse stood still, snorting an
blowing. Dusty let the rope fall from his hands, snapped:

"Get that hoss into the empty corral there. Take its saddle
off and leave it."

With that he ran to his uncle's side and dropped to his
knees. The other men of the ranch crew came crowding
forward. Dusty felt relieved to find that his uncle was still
breathing and made no attempt to move the rancher. Dusty
did not know how much or how little damage had been
done by the fall and he would not take the chance of aggra-
vating the injuries by unnecessary movement.

"How is he, Dusty?" a hand asked.

"I don't know," Dusty replied. "Keep back, all of you. Tex,
go to the house and fetch some blankets. Tell Tommy what's
happened and he'll give you what you need." He looked to
where Red was turning the paint loose in the empty corral.
"Red!" he yelled.

"Yo!" Red called back, and returned, leaving Kiowa to
move the gate poles back into place.

"Throw a saddle on that claybank of yours and head for
town. Don't go to sleep on the way. Get Doc Gorman and
happy out here."

"Is it bad?" Red asked, hesitating for a moment before
obeying Dusty's orders.

"Looks that way. Stay on in town and I'll send word as
soon as I know. Happen it is bad, you'll have to send Cousin
Betty a telegraph message and let her know. I'd not want her
bothering, so you'd best wait until you hear." Red turned
and went, taking a hand with him to help saddle the horse
with as little wasted time as possible. "Billy Jack," Dusty
went on, "take the best harness horses from the stable and
lead them halfway to Polveroso, relay teams for the Doc
when he comes."

Red and the cowhand made a record for speed in saddling and bridling a horse. The big claybank stallion, a horse
of yellowish mixture of dun and sorrel, was of little use for
cattle work. It was held in the stables behind the house as
Red's go-to-town horse and it could eat distance, run like a
scared pronghorn antelope. Red was pleased he'd taken it
as his own mount when his brothers offered him the pick of
their horses on his return from the war.

With the saddle on, Red went afork the claybank in bound and headed out of the stable. The horse was runnin at a mile-eating half gallop, a pace it could hold to Polveros with no trouble at all.

Even as he urged the horse on, Red was worried. It was a very well for Cousin Dusty to talk about not letting Cousi Betty know until they were sure how bad Ole Devil wa Betty Hardin was Ole Devil's granddaughter and, along wit Dusty, the apple of the rancher's eye. She was an orphan, black-haired, beautiful, small, and vivacious girl who, whe not at school in Memphis, ruled on OD Connected with a iron hand. She was hot-tempered, like her grandfather, an Red knew Betty would be considerably riled if she did n hear straight off about Ole Devil's accident. If Betty got rile Red was going to be the one who caught most of her tempe and that he did not want. Betty Hardin could command flow of invective as blistering as Dusty's most inspired utte ances and almost catching up to Ole Devil's violent flo Red did not want it piling on his head. He decided to sen Betty a message as soon as he's seen Hondo Fog and th doctor. He could tell Betty of the accident, that he did n know how serious it was, and promise to notify her as soo as there was something definite known. That way he wou keep himself safe and both his impulsive cousins happy.

Back at the ranch Dusty was rolling a blanket to make pillow for the rancher's head. Gently pillowing Ole Devil head, Dusty used the rest of the blankets to cover th rancher. Ole Devil's breathing was shallow now, but Dus made no attempt to move him. Looking up, Dusty told th men to get on with the work they'd been allocated the prev ous night. The new horses must be ridden and have th bedsprings worked out of their bellies, then they must l put up for a choosing match, allowing the cowhands to pi their mounts.

Kiowa took the other hands to where the remuda w held by the OD Connected wrangler and they moved th bunch of horses some distance from the house so the nois would not disturb their injured boss. Dusty stayed with h uncle, and Tommy Okasi came from the house. The tw

en stayed on either side of the rancher, neither moving
ɐy more than was necessary, watching for some sign.

Time dragged by on leaden feet. Dusty knew how long it
as likely to take Red to reach Polveroso and for the doctor
 make the ride out to the ranch. He was pleased that he'd
ought to send a team of horses to relay the doctor's buggy
alfway from town. Even with the time to change teams, the
ɪggy would make a far better speed with fresh horses.

For the first time in his life Dusty felt helpless. He could
ave handled the setting of a broken leg or arm; at a pinch
ɛ might even have chanced digging a bullet out; but this
as beyond his capabilities. He looked across the range to
here the cowhands were riding the new horses. This
ɪould have been a wild and hilarious time, good fun to be
ɪared by all, serious business treated in a lighthearted way.
here was no fun or enjoyment this day. Not with Ole Devil
ing seriously injured. Even a man being thrown in a wild
ɪcking fit did not bring the customary friendly jeers and
ɪpracticable advice usually given.

At the first sight of the distant buggy Dusty sent Tommy
kasi to fetch four cowhands from the remuda, four men of
ɪe same height. Then Tommy went to the house ready to
repare Ole Devil's room.

The other hands drifted back from the remuda as they
ɪw the approaching buggy, and Dusty did not object. He
ɪew he was going to need some more help, and the men all
anted to know how Ole Devil was. He told Kiowa to fetch a
retcher to carry Ole Devil into the house on.

The buggy came nearer. Dusty was relieved to see his
ɪother sitting beside the doctor and his father riding with
ɪlly Jack just behind the fast-rolling buggy. He'd not ex-
ɛcted Doc Gorman to make such good time and saw that
ɪnding this relay team made all the difference.

"Kiowa," Dusty called as the lean, Indian-dark hand came
ɪck with the shutter. "Take a couple of the men and tend to
ɪe doc's buggy. Walk the horses until they cool, then put
ɪem in a stable."

"Yo!" Kiowa replied, and told the men what he wanted.

There was no argument or discussion of his right to gi▸
orders. Not when Dusty told him to make the orders.

The buggy came to a halt. Doc Gorman, lean, tanned, ar▸
wearing range clothes, swung down, reaching for his b▸
while Hondo Fog left his horse and helped Mrs. Fog to g▸
down. Dusty's mother was a tall, good-looking woma▸
whose hair, what showed from under her sunbonnet, w▸
still black, untouched by gray. Her eyes were the Hard▸
black, but they were gentler than Ole Devil's. Right now h▸
face was showing anxiety, for she was very fond of h▸
brother, Ole Devil.

The doctor was looking grim as he came forward. He▸
been friend and drinking, hunting, fishing, and lie-swappi▸
companion for more years than he cared to remember, a▸
had only stayed on in the Rio Hondo during the war b▸
cause he lost a cut of the cards on whether he should ▸
with the Texas Light or stay on at home. He was known fro▸
one end of the Rio Hondo country to the other as a fi▸
hound-dog handler, a .44-caliber coon hunter, a fisherma▸
who would take a bass when no bass could be taken—and▸
real good doctor.

"Haven't moved him, have you, boy?" Gorman growled ▸
he came up.

"Nope, just pillowed his head and covered him with ▸
blanket," Dusty answered, feeling no annoyance that th▸
doctor should think he'd make such an elementary mistak▸
"What can I do now, Doc?"

"Nothing, boy. Just pull back to the corral edge with th▸
rest of the hands. Keep them out of my hair," Gorman r▸
plied, then looked at Mrs. Fog. "Bessie Mae, you come a▸
lend a hand."

Dusty withdrew, allowing his mother and the doctor ▸
make an investigation of the possible extent of the injuri▸
Hondo Fog joined his son and jerked a head toward the s▸
form on the ground:

"What happened, boy?"

"Uncle Devil tried to ride the paint there. It fought buc▸
ing straight away and piled him."

That was all Hondo Fog needed to be told. He'd seen th▸

g paint in passing and knew the danger of being thrown
m a straight bucker. He looked at Ole Devil and shook his
ad; that looked like a real bad pileup.

Gorman came to his feet, his face set in hard lines as he
lled for the stretcher. He nodded in approval as he saw
e men Dusty selected to carry the injured rancher. The
y was real capable, he must have been worried almost
ck over his uncle, but he still acted coolly and did every-
ing right. Carefully Gorman and the men lifted Ole Devil's
ill form onto the stretcher, then, under growled warnings
make sure they kept it even, the men lifted.

"Walk easy, damn you!" growled Gorman. "Don't shake
e stretcher."

"How is he, Doc?" Dusty asked.

"Bad, boy. I don't know for sure how bad. One thing I do
ow, you'll be handling the spread for a long time."

Dusty followed the stretcher bearers to the porch and
atched them start to carry Ole Devil upstairs to the bed-
om. Then he sat down in a chair on the porch to wait out
e long time until he could learn how badly Ole Devil had
en injured. He watched the four cowhands come from the
ouse, followed by Tommy Okasi. In all the time he'd known
e little Oriental, Dusty could not remember ever seeing
ommy show so much emotion. Dusty came to his feet and
id his hand on Tommy's shoulder. They did not speak;
ere was no need; both knew how the other felt. Telling
ommy to fetch Hondo a drink, Dusty turned back to his
uty as ranch *segundo*.

It was night before Gorman made more than a brief ap-
earance from the sick room, and Dusty's mother had never
ome out, her meals being taken in to her. The ranch crew
athered down by the corrals, standing in silent groups.
here was none of the usual rowdy fun in the air. The OD
onnected men, like most cowhands, liked their fun to be
ninhibited, raw, and rowdy, but not with their boss lying in
ed and not knowing if he would live or not. A pall of gloom
ung over the ranch house, the very silence a tribute to the
espect Ole Devil inspired among his men.

Dusty rose from his seat on the porch and Red Blaze

swung down from the rail of the porch. He couldn't sta[nd]
being in town and not knowing, so returned after telegra[ph]
ing the news to his cousin Betty. The redbone bitch rubb[ed]
up against Dusty and tried to wag her tail; it was almost a[s]
she knew things were bad wrong. He dropped his hand [to]
rub the bitch's long ears, then looked at Gorman and aske[d]

"How is he?"

"Bad, Dusty, bad. He'll live, but he'll never walk again. [His]
back's broken."

Dusty stood rigid, his face fighting down any emotion. [At]
his side he heard Red suck his breath in and let it out aga[in]
in a long gust. The two men tried to fight down their distre[ss]
at the news, and the two redbones, as if knowing the tra[gic]
news, rubbed up against Dusty and Red for sympathy. Dus[ty]
could hardly believe it was possible that Ole Devil Hard[in]
would never walk again, never lead his men to work or w[ar]
again.

"There's no way we can get him back on his feet again[?]"
Dusty asked.

"If there was, I'd be doing it right now."

"How about in the East?" Red inquired. "In one of tho[se]
big city hospitals, there might be—"

"No chance of it, Red boy," Gorman replied, not annoy[ed]
at the words. He knew there was no slighting of his ability [as]
a doctor. It was just that the two young men wanted eve[ry]
thing possible to be done for their uncle. "Even if we co[uld]
get him to one alive—and that's not likely—it wouldn't [do]
any good."

"Is he conscious?" Dusty asked.

"Yes."

"Does he know about it?"

Gorman shook his head. "I haven't told him yet, boy[s. I]
want you to tell him."

"Me!" Dusty spat the word out. "Doc, you can't ask me [to]
go in there and tell Uncle Devil he'll never walk again."

Before Gorman could answer this, the ranch door open[ed]
again and Mrs. Fog came out. She knew what Gorman w[as]
asking Dusty and knew her brother would rather get [the]
news from Dusty than from any other living soul. It wa[s]

ard thing for her son to do, but she knew Dusty would do

"Devil's asking for you, Dustine," she said. "You'd best go p and see him."

Reluctantly Dusty went into the house, across the large ntrance hall, and up the stairs. He paused at the top of the airs, but Gorman gently laid a hand on his shoulder and queezed it. Dusty took a deep breath and went to the door f Ole Devil's bedroom. He opened the door and stepped side, his eyes going to the bed, lit by a lamp set on the edside table.

Ole Devil lay stiff and rigid in the bed, the blankets drawn p almost to his chin. His body was wrapped tightly in ban-ages to prevent any movement that might further injure is spine. For all that his eyes were open and despite being ulled with pain, they focused on Dusty. There was some of he old fire left in the voice as Ole Devil barked:

"I want to know how I am, Dusty."

"Yes, sir," Dusty replied, standing at a rigid brace, his ands clenched so tight that the knuckles showed white. He ried to speak but could not bring the words out.

"Captain Fog!" Ole Devil's voice took on a note Dusty new all too well. "I want you to tell me now. I'd rather have from you than anybody."

"You're hurt bad, sir," Dusty said huskily, fighting to keep ny sign of emotion out of his voice. "Wouldn't you rather ait until morning, sir?"

"Would I be any different than?"

Once more Dusty did not answer immediately. He saw le Devil's eyes flash in sudden annoyance and knew any elay in answering would bring to a boil that hot and irasci-le temper. It would not be advisable in Ole Devil's state to llow him to get angry.

"No, sir," Dusty replied. Once more he took a deep breath nd went on. "Your back's broken. You'll never walk again."

Ole Devil's eyes closed as he lay still for a long minute. It as to be the hardest fight of his life, and there was nothing nyone could do to help him. Dusty stood rigid, unmoving, ardly breathing, trying to think of words to say that might

ease the blow. Finally the eyes opened and Hardin looke
up at Dusty's face.

"It looks like you and young Red'll be left to run the plac
for quite a spell, boy. Allow you can handle it."

"We'll surely make a try, sir. Doc might be wrong abou
your not walking again."

"I doubt it, boy. He might not know sic 'em about han
dling a hound dog, but there's not many who can touch hir
in the doctoring line," grunted Ole Devil. "Soon as I can ge
out of the bed, we'll get me a wheelchair, and I'll do all I ca
to help run the spread from it. It might mean that you hav
to stay home and let one of the other men handle the floa
ing outfit we were going to start."

Dusty nodded his agreement. The floating outfit wa
something he and Ole Devil had planned, a kind of mobi
ranch crew, working away from the main spread, five or s
men and a cook handling work that was too far from th
home spread for the main crew to handle. Dusty thought h
would lead the floating outfit while Ole Devil took comman
of the local work. Now it looked as if he would have
shelve the idea, or let one of the other men handle it.

"How's the paint?" Ole Devil asked.

"He's all right. We took the saddle off and put him back
the breaking pen. There's some of the boys who wanted
shoot him."

"Like hell!" barked Ole Devil. "That hoss's got to
whipped, Dusty. No hoss can lick our clan."

"I'll tend to it, sir," promised Dusty.

"Watch him when he goes up for the sixth jump, boy.
uses the other five to build himself up for that one," warne
Ole Devil. "He'll take some riding, boy."

Dusty nodded, then turned and left the room. One thi
Dusty knew, he was going to ride and master that paint
get killed trying.

On the following morning Dusty was early in the stab
His saddle hung over a burro, a structure shaped like
inverted A. The burro was a stand for saddles, for no co
hand would want to leave the most valuable item of h
worldly goods lying on the ground where it might be da

ed. If possible he would always try to leave the saddle
ver a burro and out of harm's way. He did not take the
ouble-girthed saddle immediately, but examined it with
re. First he checked that the insides of the stirrup irons
ere smooth and there was nothing to prevent a speedy
ithdrawal of the foot from them. Next he checked the
rths, changing one that was slightly frayed.

Red Blaze came in, watching the preparations and ap-
roving them. He jerked his thumb over his shoulder.

"We've got the paint caught ready, Dusty. I'll tote your
addle down for you."

The big paint stood as on the previous day, allowing men
saddle, bridle, and blindfold it. Every hand, from Billy
ack to the cook, were lining the sorrel rails ready to give
eir vocal encouragement to Dusty in his ride. There was a
onsiderable amount of money bet on the result of the ride,
usty guessed, as he went forward. He checked the
eatherwork of the horse, making sure everything was as he
anted it. Then he swung into the double-girthed rig and
ettled down. His knees gripped the saddle and he felt the
ig horse tense. Dusty gave Red the sign to jerk away the
lindfold, then get clear. He felt as if he was sat on a keg of
unpowder with a fuse lit, waiting for the explosion. Any
oment now, even as Red pulled clear the blindfold and
ved from the corral, the explosion was going to come.

It did.

The big horse came up off the ground in a straight-away
uck that went higher than Dusty could ever remember go-
g on a horse before. Dusty rode the high buck jumps with
o great difficulty. He was a skilled horse buster and pos-
essed the rare sixth sense that enabled him to guess which
ay the horse was going next. His early riding training and
is jujitsu lessons from Tommy Okasi caused him to lose
ny fear of falling, and he knew how to light down rolling,
nding with as little damage as possible. His quirt was on
is wrist, his hat set firmly on his head, and his Kelly spurs
aking the horse at every jump as he concentrated on keep-
g the paint's head up. He knew that the horse must not be
llowed to take charge of the fight.

Suddenly, without any warning, the paint changed fightin style. The straight bucks became close-to-the-ground leap The paint went fast, not leaping high, but keeping close t the ground, kicking sideways with his hindquarters as h shook his head and appeared to be trying to explode him self into separate pieces. The savage fury of the horse ca ried it the length of the breaking pen, then it changed direc tion and came back, still fighting close to the ground. It wa a fast-moving, deadly effective way of fighting; the pai knew just what it aimed to do.

Then it did it.

For a brief instant Dusty lost all idea of which way th horse was going, the sudden change in fighting styles havin taken him completely by surprise. He lost contact with th horse and knew what to expect next. Dusty took the eas way out. He'd lost the saddle and one stirrup, so he kicke the other foot free and went sailing through the air to lan rolling.

Dusty heard the scared yells of the hands and did not tr to stop his roll. He went through the corral rails, hearing smashing thud just over his head. Then he looked up at th at-first-anxious, then grinning faces. He sat up, his eyes g ing to Red's face as that worthy was looking at the fence rai Getting up, Dusty joined his cousin and looked down. Dee in the wood at the bottom rail was the imprint of the paint iron-shod hoof. His head must have been just underneat when the paint slashed down; only the stout timber ha saved him.

"Wowee, Red!" said Dusty, running his finger around th groove. "I tell you, that's a tolerable fierce horse."

Even though he had won twenty dollars betting Dusty g piled once, Billy Jack looked miserable as he walked up.

"What are you doing down there?" he asked mildly. "Th hoss's in thar."

"Why, sure," Dusty agreed. "My hat came off and I g down to chase it."

The other hands gave derisive whoops and laughs at th time-worn excuse for being thrown from a horse. Then Re and Kiowa went in to rope the big horse and move it ba to the bronc stall, where the blindfold was put on once more. Dusty tested his limbs to make sure they were all working, then called:

"Bring him out, Cousin Red. I'll give him another whirl."

The men knew Dusty would go right back and try again. To let a horse get away with piling his rider too often was bad. It gave the horse bad ideas. So any horse buster worth his salt would, if not badly injured, get back on and have another try as soon as he could.

"Reckon we should put a buck strap on the saddle, Dusty?" a cowhand yelled.

Dusty grinned and ignored the remark. The buck strap was a strip of leather that was sometimes riveted to the saddle housing, just below the base at the offside of the horn, and used as a handhold to help stay mounted during the bucking. It was a thing that no cowhand worth his salt would use, feeling it was cissified. Dusty was a horse buster of the first water and proud of it; he would never use a buck strap. However, the suggestion was always made when a good rider was thrown and went back for a second try.

Once more Dusty swung afork the big paint and the blindfold was removed. The savage fight resumed with the fury that had marked the first bout. The big paint fought like a demon and changed his fighting style fast and regular in a way that not one horse in a thousand learned to do. It bucked straight away, then switched to close-to-the-ground work, but Dusty rode the wild pitching, raking with his spurs and encouraging the horse to greater efforts. Through the repertoire of bucking, the big paint ran, showing more styles than two different horses usually knew. It changed styles, in fishing, twisting its body in a crescent, alternatively to the right then to the left, looking as if trying to touch the ground with first one then the other shoulder and letting the sunlight hit its belly each time: crawfishing, cowhopping, fence worming, the big paint did them all, but Dusty kept in the saddle and his spurs raked home.

Up on its hind legs reared the paint, chinning the moon, forefeet flailing the air. Dusty reversed his quirt and brought the loaded end down between the horse's ears and batted

down. Cinch binding, rearing like that, was deadly dange
ous to both horse and rider, for the horse was likely to g
backward, which would not do it any good. It wouldn't mak
the rider feel too good either. The horse came down on a
four feet, then started to fight again.

On the corral rails the OD Connected men were silen
watching a savage and primeval battle between a man and
magnificent horse. The hands' excited cheers and yells wer
silent now; they just watched, trying to remember a hors
ride to equal this battle.

Then it was over. The churned-up dust of the breakin
pen began to settle down, and the big horse stood wit
hanging head and sweat-soaked sides heaving. Dusty sat th
saddle leaning forward and gasping for breath. He felt as
every inch of his body had been pounded to a pulp, bu
he'd won. To make sure, he raked the horse with his spur
The big horse made a game try at fighting again, then cam
to a halt, and a further scratching with the spurs brought n
response.

Dusty slid from the saddle, gasping for breath. The fir
stage of the training of the paint was over. The horse now
knew one man was its master. Dusty stroked the big horse
sweat-lathered neck, gasping out derisive but kindly word
that calmed the quivering horse.

Red came running forward and took the paint's reins, t
walk the horse until it cooled, and Dusty walked slowly t
the corral fence, sinking down to sit on the bottom rail.
was the hardest, toughest, and most satisfying ride he'd eve
had.

In the following days Dusty spent all his spare time wit
the paint. He was compelled to take the bedsprings out o
the horse for the first three days after his original successf
ride. Slowly, kindness and firm handling showed their r
sults and the paint accepted Dusty as its master. For a tim
Dusty rode the horse around the breaking pen, then starte
to use it on the circle, riding the range. He planned to mak
the horse his personal mount and, to show Red and th
others they were wrong in their judgment of paints, to trai
the horse for cattle work.

Ten days went by. Ole Devil was still bedridden but getting slowly stronger. Word reached the ranch that Betty Harman was finished with school and coming home to take charge of the house. The news was greeted with mixed feelings, for Betty ran the spread with an iron hand. Billy Jack moaned at the news.

"If one of them ain't enough, we got to have two," he wailed in the bunkhouse. "What with that mean ole Dusty rousing us to work all day and Betty chousing us at night to keep the hawg pen looking tidy, we ain't never going to have no peace."

Billy Jack got little sympathy. He was always the same when caught for his turn on the blister end of a shovel, clearing water holes or digging stumps.

Ole Devil was resigned to the thought that he'd never walk again and he looked forward. He planned to have a wheelchair, make his bedroom on the ground floor and save going up or downstairs. He received a report from Dusty every day on the running of the ranch and the progress in taming the paint. Ole Devil felt no resentment at Dusty's breaking the paint, only pride at the youngster's achievement.

Dusty's other news was in one way heartening, in another gave Ole Devil a lot of worry. Dusty had returned late from riding the circle on the eleventh night after riding the paint. Rather than disturb the house, he left the big stallion in the breaking pen and went to bed. The sudden crashing bellow of the two hounds woke him shortly after one o'clock.

Dusty came off his bed, pulling one of his guns as his feet hit the floor. He went to the door, opened it, and darted downstairs, hearing Red's door open and bare feet pattering on the floor behind him. Dusty did not wait; there were only two things capable of making the hounds sing out in the night: a cougar on the prowl or a man doing the same thing. Neither cougar nor man should be prowling in the dark, Dusty knew that, so his gun was cocked as he jerked open the house door and went onto the porch.

The two redbone hounds went by him, their crashing

song ringing into the air as they hurled for the breaking pe
Dusty leapt from the porch; he could see vague shapes b
the pen. Shapes that could only be men. He heard a lo
thud as the bars of the corral gate dropped, then yells an
shouts.

"Hold it!" Dusty challenged.

Flame lanced from the air as a man fired from the back c
his horse. The bullet went nowhere near Dusty, for the ma
did not know much about shooting in the dark. Dusty di
He'd made plenty of practice firing in the darkness and hi
gun roared back as he hit the ground. He rolled over as h
landed to prevent any of the men by the corral aiming at th
gunflash and hitting him. He saw one rider reeling, the
slipping down from the back of his horse. Then the other
were moving fast, breaking in different directions and ru
ning. Dusty came up, running forward, but he was too late
The big paint—spooked by the noise, the clamor of th
hounds, the shouts of the horse thieves, and the shots—
broke from the corral and went streaking across the range
running wildly away from the breaking pen.

Dusty listened to the rapidly departing hooves as th
horse thieves came together again along the Polveroso tra
and headed away from the OD Connected.

Men came streaming from the bunkhouse, and Red ra
up. Now he held a lantern in one hand, a Colt in the othe
He halted and looked at his cousin.

"They get you, Cousin Dusty?"

"Nope. I got one. He's down by the breaking pen. Th
paint's out and running."

The ranch crew expressed their anger at the words i
whatever manner they favored best. Kiowa spoke up, sayin
more than he'd done in a month:

"Want for us to take out after them, Dusty?"

"Could you trail them in the dark?" inquired Dusty.

"Nope!" Kiowa relapsed into his usual speech.

"They went along the Polveroso trail," another hand pu
in.

"Which same means they won't stick on it," Dust
drawled, thinking fast and making his plans. "Time you ge

addled they'll be long gone. Red, see Jimmo and tell him ou'll be wanting food for three men. Then come sunup, ou take Billy Jack and Kiowa. I want the men who tried to eal the paint brought back, or killed."

"We'll do that," agreed Red. "You'd best go see Uncle evil while I take a look at that *hombre* you downed. I'll ome up as soon as I've took a look."

"That'll be best," Dusty grunted. "Tell Jimmo I'll be want- ng some food at sunup. Make a separate bundle from ours. I'm going after the paint."

Dusty turned and went back into the house, going up- airs toward his uncle's room. There was a light showing nder the door, and he found Tommy Okasi already with le Devil.

The rancher lay back and listened to Dusty's story, then rowled. "You reckon young Red can handle them with only vo men?"

"Sure. There wasn't more than five men, and I got one. I eckon Kiowa and Billy Jack'll be all the help Red needs."

"How about you?" Ole Devil inquired.

"I'm going after the paint."

"Where do you allow he'll have gone?"

"Way I see it, he's scared and running. Most likely make ack for the Ronde River country. He's not been here long nough to make it his home."

Ole Devil agreed with this. A range horse would always eturn to its home if free and running. The paint would not egard the OD Connected as its home yet; later it might, but t the moment the Ronde River bottoms was what the horse emembered as home, and there the paint would be run- ing.

"It's a big area, boy."

"Yes, sir," Dusty drawled. "I hope to run the paint down efore he gets too far in. If not, I'll just have to start looking."

Red came into the room at that moment. "That hoss thief ou shot, Dusty. We recognized him. He was with the *hom- re* who wanted to buy the paint. The tent showman who ame the day Trader brought the hosses in."

"That figgers," grunted Dusty. "Put the body in the barn, Red. We'll send word to Pappy in the morning."

Red left to make the arrangements, and Ole Devil looked at Dusty. "The Ronde River country's wild, boy," he warned. "You ought to be taking more men with you."

"I'd rather play it lone-handed, sir," answered Dusty. "We need all the men on the spread."

Two days later Dusty was riding toward the Ronde River bottoms. He rode the big black stallion he'd ridden through the war, this being the only horse he thought would be able to catch the paint in a race.

CHAPTER THREE

he Ronde River bottoms was a new range to Dusty, beyond
he boundary of the OD Connected ranch. He'd found the
aint's tracks earlier that day and was riding along what he
oped was the right line. The big horse was no longer run-
ing wild but moving at an easy, mile-eating lope. By hold-
g his big black to a slightly better speed Dusty hoped to be
ble to catch sight of the paint, then move in on it.

The sudden howling of buffalo wolves brought Dusty's
orse to a halt. The young Texan reached down and loos-
ned a Spenser carbine in the saddle boot. He did not often
arry a saddle gun, having never found one that satisfied
im, but for this mission he'd thought the Spenser was ad-
isable. Right now he was pleased to have the .52-caliber,
even-shot repeating carbine with him. The buffalo wolves
ere big brutes, powerful, fast, and dangerous. A single buf-
lo wolf was capable of pulling down a young cow buffalo,
nd the wolves always ran in packs of ten or so. The only
ood thing about them was that, when hunted regularly,
ey came fast to know what the sound of a rifle meant.

The wolves were hunting. It was five years since he'd last
eard wolves baying, but it was a sound a man never forgot.
hey were running some prey, driving it before them and
aveling with that tireless loping speed that would bring
own even the fleetest game in the end. Suddenly the sound
hanged, the pitch altered, and the wolves were not chasing
ny longer, they were clamoring and baying as they cor-
ered their prey.

Dusty turned his horse toward the sound. The wolves

came from ahead of him, and that was where the big pain
had been. Putting his Kelly spurs to work, Dusty urged th
horse forward, making for the sound. He bent and pulle
the Spenser from the saddle boot, worked the lever to throv
a cartridge into the breech, but did not draw back the bi
side hammer of the gun. He urged the horse to the top o
the slope and looked down.

The paint horse was cornered in a pocket, backed into
small, steep walled gully and defending itself against half
dozen gaunt, gray shapes. The buffalo-wolf pack were show
ing some caution, slinking forward, then leaping clear of th
iron-shod hooves as the paint lashed out at them. One wo
lay back from the others, thrashing over and over in agony
sent there with a smashed back from a pile-driver kick.

Even as Dusty watched, a movement on the slope ove
the paint's head caught his eye. He looked with more care.
lean, gray shape moved through the grass to the rim of th
pocket. It was a big dog wolf, possibly the leader of the pacl
showing the savage cunning of its kind. The wolf was sneal
ing into the edge of the pocket, then would leap down onto
the horse's back, startling it and making it lunge forwar
Once it was clear of the pocket, the other wolves woul
close in. A sudden leap in, the slash of powerful jaws, an
the paint would be hamstrung, lame, and helpless.

Dusty brought the carbine up, hauling back the hamme
sighting and firing fast. There was little or no chance of a h
at that range, for the Spenser was not a weapon of accurac
over fifty yards. The bullet slapped into the brush and ricc
cheted up with a vicious whining scream, and the wo
jumped back, turning to look around. It was as Dusty hopec
He sent the big black hurling forward down the slope and le
out a wild rebel war cry. The Spenser boomed out agai
slammed lead near the wolf up on the top of the pocket.
whirled and faded into the bushes, streaking off, and th
others turned, then went like gray shadows. Dusty did no
fire again; there was no chance of his making a hit, so he di
not bother.

The big paint stood snorting in the pocket, but before
could decide to make a run for it, Dusty was in front of th

ening. He booted the carbine and quickly unstrapped the
pe. Talking gently, allowing the paint to settle down, Dusty
de nearer. The horse snorted and reared once, then be-
n to calm down, and Dusty rode straight up to it, slipping
e noose around its neck.

"Easy now, old hoss," he said gently. "Easy, you remem-
r me. We're going back home, old-timer."

Turning the black, Dusty rode from the pocket, and the
int followed him with no trouble. Dusty felt relieved. The
g paint accepted him again and did not appear to have
ne completely back to the wild. He decided against riding
e paint until he reached the Rio Hondo country and could
so in the breaking pen the first time. With that thought in
ind Dusty turned his horses back in the direction he'd
me and headed for home.

Shortly before noon the following day Dusty was riding
ong the rim of an arroyo. He was nearing the OD Con-
cted's unmarked line and relaxed in his saddle as he fol-
wed the top of the arroyo, picking it as the easiest trail. To
e left rose a steep slope and he was skirting the edge of
e scar left where a watercourse had eroded and cut into
e land; this was how an arroyo was formed. The sides
ere steeply dropped, and at the bottom, in the center of
e two walls, ran a small stream, which in time of flood
ecame a fast-running and roaring torrent, carrying the wa-
r to the Ronde River.

A man who rode the dangerous trails built up an instinct
r danger. Dusty was no exception to this rule. Something
arned him that all was not well. There was a movement,
aught in the very corner of his eye. Dusty started to twist
round; he heard the driving slap as a bullet smashed into
e big black horse, felt the black falling under him, and
cked his feet from the stirrups. To his ears came the flat,
apping crack of a Henry rifle.

Dusty pitched from his saddle as the horse went down. He
ent over to the side away from the shooter, unable to grab
is Spenser from the saddle boot as he left his horse. The
ap of a second bullet over his head warned him there was
o time to waste. He went over the edge of the arroyo,

falling and rolling down the steep side. Then he was dropping through the air, falling the last few feet to the sof sandy bottom. He lit down dazed, but shook it off fast an looked around.

The water at flood times had undercut the bank just her slashing under all the way along the arroyo side. Dusty sa why he'd fallen through space for the last feet of his roll safety. Saw it and knew its advantage. He dived under th cutback, out of sight from the rim above, even as he hear the sound of approaching horses. The first thing Dusty di was check his weapons. The two Colts had been held b their restraining straps in the holsters, but they'd picked u some dirt and grit on the roll down the slope. Quickly Dust pulled the first Colt and turned the chamber after setting th hammer at half cock. Not for the first time in his life Dust felt grateful to old Colonel Sam for designing such goo weapons. It took more than a bit of dirt and grit to put th old army Colt out of whack. The second Colt would also fir Dusty was sure of that. He holstered both weapons and gav thought to his situation. There was at least one Henry rif up on the rim, and a Henry would outrange an army Col Dusty was safe unless the man who had shot his horse an tried to kill him moved along the rim top and got into place on a curve where he could see under the cutback.

On the rim above, four men rode down the slope towar the paint and the dead black. One of them was Covacs, th tent showman. He grinned savagely as he came toward th big paint, his Henry rifle smoking in his hands. The othe three men were from his show, men he'd selected fro among a hardcase crew to help steal the horse. The failu of the raid and the knowledge that the paint had broken o had brought Covacs and his men to the Ronde River cou try, for they knew, as did Dusty, that the horse would mal for its home range. They'd taken a roundabout route, ho ing to shake off any pursuit from the OD Connected. Cova had seen Dusty riding the edge of the arroyo and laid ambush. He'd hoped to get the young Texan, but only kill the horse, and now Dusty was down at the bottom of th arroyo, alive and still dangerous.

"We'll have to get him," Covacs remarked.

There was no argument to the words. They were stealing horse and there was a witness who could see them all ang for it. There was only one snag to removing the wit- ss. He was Dusty Fog. Even in the early days Dusty's skill th his matched guns was known, talked about. No man of erage talent with a gun was willing to chance matching ots with Dusty Fog.

One of the men looked down the arroyo sides, peeking utiously over the top. He jerked his head back, face white.

"He ain't down there!"

"What?" Covacs snarled, and peered over himself.

Covacs was pale under his tan as he saw the sign below d tried to guess how Dusty had disappeared. One thing he d not need to guess. Any man who went to the bottom of e arroyo without suitable covering fire was going to get art, and fast. He most likely wouldn't even know what had t him, for he'd be sliding down into easy range of the xan's guns.

There was indecision on the faces of the other three men. vacs saw it and knew why. The men were brave enough hen handling a booze-blind mark who complained about ing taken for his roll. Facing a man like Dusty Fog was mething different. The Texan must be removed, that was r sure. He would never rest until he'd got the men who led one of his horses and tried to steal the other.

"We've got to take him," Covacs growled. "I'll take the ss back to Hagen City and wait for the show to catch up ith me. You three get him. There'll be a hundred dollars for ch of you if you bring me his gunbelt and guns."

The three men looked at each other. Then one growled, eave us that Henry and we'll make us a try."

"I'll do that," Covacs agreed, handing the rifle over and gging out a box of bullets. "Just let me get the hoss and art out."

The paint allowed the men to approach. Covacs tossed his pe over the sleek neck and one of the others severed usty's lariat, cutting the paint free from the dead black. he paint knew better than to try to fight a rope and followed Covacs as he rode away from the edge of the arroyo up the slope and out of sight.

The three men watched their boss ride away, then looked down into the arroyo bottom. They could not think where Dusty had gone and that worried them. Not one of them spoke for some time, then one growled, "We'd best try and get it started."

"Sure," the one with the Henry remarked. "Bill, go up there to the right apiece, then slide down to the bottom. Me 'n' Lippy'll head off down the other way. He'll go down to the bottom with his Sharps carbine and I'll stop up here ready to cover you with the Henry."

The other two did not care for the idea of going down the arroyo bottom, not with Dusty Fog waiting, but they could not offer any better idea. One thing was for sure, Dusty Fog would have to show himself when they were down and the Henry rifle would cut him down.

Dusty was waiting under the cutback, cold rage gripping him, yet not making him forget to think. The big black had been his favorite horse, the mount that he rode throughout the war, and those men, whoever they were, had killed a good horse without a second thought. They'd also stolen the paint and they'd be coming down after him, that was for sure.

With that in mind Dusty started to move along the bottom of the arroyo, keeping out of sight under the cutback. A scattering of dirt came over the edge of the cutback and Dusty froze. He looked back and gauged how far he'd come. The man on top of the slope would not risk coming down yet, that was certain. Slowly Dusty moved on, trying to keep up with the man above. Then he saw more stones and dirt rattling down and knew the man was sliding down. Dusty did not draw his guns; he wanted the man alive if possible.

A pair of feet came into sight; the man evidently did not know about the cutback. Dusty grabbed the ankles and pulled hard. He heard a startled yell, the bark of a shot, and the man came crashing down. Dusty wasted no time; he lunged forward even as the man landed on hands and knees at the foot of the slope. Dusty rolled the man over and

mashed up a punch that lifted him almost to his feet, then
umped him down flat on his back. The man lay still, but
usty knew he was far from being out of the tall timber.
nother man was sliding down the slope, back along the
raw, a man who held a Sharps carbine. The man was fifty
ards away, well beyond normal handgun range, and Dusty
new his only chance was to make a hit real fast, before the
han could get his balance. The Sharps toter was looking
oward Dusty even now and the young Texan knew he
vould be living on borrowed time the minute the other man
ot set to shoot.

With a rolling dive Dusty went behind the unconscious
ictim of his attack. He brought out the right-handed Colt,
ripped the butt firmly, and with both hands pulled back the
ammer. Resting his wrists on the man's body Dusty laid his
ights with care. He knew the Colt, knew its vagaries, and
llowed for them as he sighted. The Colt kicked back against
is hands; he saw the man staggered by his bullet, dropping
he Sharps. Even so, he was only hit high in the shoulder
nd was still a potential danger. Dusty lunged up, running
orward to get into better range before the man could re-
over and bring up the Sharps carbine again.

It was then Dusty saw the third man still on the rim. If
usty had stayed at the side, the man could not have seen
im. Right now Dusty was out in the open and the man lined
is Henry rifle down. At that range if the man was anything
f a shot, he could not miss. It was a range where a man
ould do nothing in offhand shooting with a revolver.

The man's Henry slanted down, then he looked away
rom the arroyo bottom and swung the rifle around to fire at
omeone or something that was coming toward him and out
f Dusty's sight. At the flat bark of the Henry there was a
nore distant bellow from a Spenser carbine. The man spun
round, his Henry falling from his hands as he pitched over
he edge of the arroyo and crashed to the bottom.

The wounded man was on his knees, lining the Sharps
arbine on Dusty, but the killing of his friend put his aim off.
usty ran forward, then halted and started to throw fast
hots. The army Colt sounded like a thunderclap in the nar-

row confines of the arroyo. On the third shot the ma
reared up, his carbine fell, and he jerked as another bull
smashed into him. Then he went down.

Dusty did not wait; he flung himself back into the shelte
of the cutback. He did not know who'd killed the man wit
the Henry, but there were a number of possibilities, none
them pleasant to a man with only five bullets left. A voic
came floating down and Dusty could not remember whe
Red Blaze sounded so welcome.

"You all right, Cousin Dusty?"

Dusty holstered his guns and stepped out. Red, Billy Jacl
and Kiowa sat their horses at the edge of the arroyo, lookin
down with broad grins on their faces.

"Sure, I'm all right. Throw me a rope down and haul m
up."

Billy Jack's rope dropped and Dusty climbed up. At th
top he looked at the dead black and the severed rope an
gave a low curse. His eyes went to the nickeled Henry an
he swore he'd never rest until he put Covacs under.

"What happened?" asked Red.

Dusty explained and there were angry curses from two
the others. Kiowa was never the man to waste his words. H
rode his horse along the rim and used his rope to slid
down to where Dusty's first victim was groaning to co
sciousness again. The lean man fastened his rope under th
man's arms, then climbed up and hauled the man out with
out any ceremony. While Kiowa was performing this act
kindness, Red told Dusty how they'd been on the trail of th
gang, following the roundabout route taken by the hors
thieves, and they came up in time to see the man lining h
Henry on the bottom of the arroyo. This, taken with th
shots and the dead black, told Red all he wanted to kno
and he cut in fast. His Spenser answered the Henry cha
lenge and Dusty knew the rest.

"We've got to get Covacs," Dusty remarked, his voic
grim. "He's not got much of a start on us."

"Got enough," growled Red. "It'll be dark before we ca
catch up with him and, like you told us, we can't run a line i
the darkness."

"Lookee here, Dusty," Billy Jack went on. "We got us a an here who knows where that Covacs went. I know you don't go for no torturing prisoners and such, but just this ace you can look the other way. This gent knows where 's got to meet his boss; he might just tell us."

"How about it?" Red asked the prisoner, who was on his et and looking sullen.

"Go to hell!"

"And meet your two pards?" Red said, and pulled back his t.

"That's a slow way," grunted Kiowa. He was rarely a man ho said much and when he did he was mostly well worth tening to.

Taking his rope, Kiowa tossed the loop about the man's eck and with a twist of his wrist drew the *honda* tight under e man's left ear. Then he moved in and before the man uld object or struggle, pigging-thonged his hands behind s back. Stepping back, Kiowa surveyed his handiwork. They allus hangs hoss thieves, don't they?" he asked.

"Ain't no tree within a couple of miles," Billy Jack pointed ut.

Kiowa grunted, as if disappointed that his friend thought e'd miss such an elementary thing. He fastened the free nd of the rope to his saddle horn and pushed the man ward the edge of the arroyo. The man tried to struggle, ut he was like a child in Kiowa's hands. His face paled and e felt his feet scrabbling the very edge of the arroyo.

"You'd best talk, friend," Billy Jack remarked dolefully. Ole Kiowa'll push you over and think nothing of it."

"Stop him!" the man screamed. "Stop him! I'll talk. I'll tell ou. Covac's gone to Hagen City. He took the paint and we'd ot to meet him there."

Kiowa allowed the man to come back from the edge and ooked at Dusty, who was moving forward. "He telling the uth, you reckon?" Kiowa asked.

"Sure, I reckon he is."

"Don't need him anymore, then, do we?" said Kiowa ildly, and pushed the man.

Dusty leapt forward. He was only just in time; the man

was teetering on the very edge of the arroyo. Another se ond and the man would have gone over, the rope snappir tight under his ear and breaking his neck.

"You crazy Indian!" Dusty barked at the unabashed K owa.

"Spoilsport," replied Kiowa. "We never said we wouldr hang him after he told us."

"We'll take him with us," Dusty drawled. "Happen he's lie to us we'll still have him to make sorry for it."

...to bring his (?) to the very edge of the arroyo. Another
...od and the man would have gone over the rim. Then grip-
...with savage power, and breaking his neck
...or Covacs now. Dusty barely had time...

CHAPTER FOUR

...vacs walked to the livery-barn corral in the early morn-
...g. The corral was empty and there was no one in sight. He
...ld a stiff, brutal whip in his right hand, a length of thin
...rd in his left, and there was a sadistic gleam in his eyes as
... looked at the big paint in the corral.

"You big devil," he snarled. "Time I've done with you and
...u've had the whip and ghost cord, you'll not let any man
...le you."

Covacs was about to climb into the corral when he heard
...e sound of hooves. A soft drawled voice came to his ears
...d froze him to the spot.

"I've been looking for you, Covacs."

The showman turned, his face turning pale and his tongue
...ing to wet lips that were suddenly dry.

The small Texan, who should have been lying dead in the
...nely arroyo, stood just behind him. Three hard-faced
...xas cowhands sat behind the youngster and beyond
...em, bound to his horse was one of Covacs's men. There
...ere two tarp-wrapped shapes across the back of another
...rse, which explained where the other two men were.

Covacs watched Dusty's hands, knew how little chance he
...uld stand in a gunfight.

"Count to five, Cousin Red," Dusty said gently. "Start
...en you like, Covacs. I start at five."

Covacs licked his lips. This was a challenge and held a
...adly warning. Dusty was giving him the first break, al-
...wing him to make the first move—but at the count of five

Dusty meant to draw whether Covacs was making a move not.

Slowly the showman lowered his left hand to unbuckle gunbelt and throw it behind him. It fell inside the corral a the big paint stood snorting in anger as if it knew the fa the man had planned for it.

"You lousy, yeller-gutted, hoss-killing skunk!" Red Bla hissed, and swung down from his saddle, his hands going his belt buckle.

"He's mine, Red!" Dusty's voice was soft and gentle, y there was deadly menace in it. *"Hombre,* you killed r horse and stole this paint. I'm going to beat you until you wished you'd drawn."

Covacs snorted, watching Dusty moving closer. "I'm gentleman. I do not brawl like a common cowhand."

He started to turn, then swung back, his fist smashing into Dusty's face. The small Texan was knocked backwa and Covacs leapt in smashing another punch, whi knocked Dusty down. The showman leapt forward, his fo lifting to stomp down. Covacs gave a yell as two han caught his down-swinging foot and twisted it. The streng of the young Texan took him by surprise. Dusty forced hi self to his knees, still holding the foot, then lunged up a shoved hard. Covacs yelled as he crashed into the cor fence. His hand gripped the butt of the whip and as he car up, the lash leapt out, biting into Dusty's flesh.

Three times the whip hit home; then, as it was driving o for the fourth, Dusty's hand shot down and caught the las Gripping the leather, Dusty pulled with all his streng Covacs gave a startled yell as he was dragged forwa Dusty let loose of the whip and drove his right fist into t big man's stomach, smashing home the blow with all t power in his frame. The big man doubled over and went his knees, both hands clutching his stomach.

Dusty's knees smashed up, driving with all his power in Covacs's face, smashing the nose. Blood gushed out, thic ening in the heavy mustache as the man was lifted almost his feet. Dusty followed up the attack with hard-swu punches that ripped the big man's face, smashed his hea

m side to side, and drove him reeling toward the corral
e.

Covacs staggered before the savage attack. He turned and
v his gun, forgot where it lay, and dived over the corral
l, landing on the ground, rolled over, and brought the
volver from his holster. Even as he started to lift the
apon, Covacs heard a yell of warning, the thunder of
oves, and the fighting scream of an enraged horse. He
sted around and screamed aloud as he saw the big paint
ring over him with hooves slashing and ripping down.

Too late Covacs tried to avoid the horse. One great hoof
ashed onto his head; then as he fell the paint was on him,
ping home savage kicks that tore open the man's head as
t were paper.

Dusty lunged forward but Red and Billy Jack threw them-
ves on him and held him back. It would be certain death
go into the corral while the horse was filled with bloodlust
d fighting mad.

'It's too late, Dusty," Billy Jack drawled gently. "You can't
a thing."

"What a way to go," Dusty answered, standing still.

'No more'n he asked for," growled Billy Jack, and picked
the thin, strong piece of cord. "He aimed to use this on
horse."

Dusty took the cord, the ghost cord, that instrument of
ture used only by the most callous and brutal of horse-
eakers. The cord would have been fastened around the
rse's tongue and gums, the ends carried back and used as
ns, inflicting terrible pain to the animal. The pain would
her turn the paint into a vicious and unmanageable killer
break its spirit. That was how a man like Covacs treated a
rse. He would never do it again.

Dusty watched the big horse for a moment and then
ped through the corral rails and walked forward. All the
e he went toward the horse, he spoke gently, showing no
n of fear. Slowly the big horse drew back from the bloody
ng that once was a man. For a moment the watching men
ught the horse would charge, and Red dropped his hand
his side, ready to draw and shoot. Then the horse re-

171

laxed, the wild fury leaving its eyes. Dusty went straight
the horse and stroked its sleek neck. He knew he'd won; th
paint was his.

Red Blaze, Billy Jack, and Kiowa stood watching. The
could hear the sound of running feet as men came to inve
tigate the noise. Kiowa grunted, his eyes on Dusty and th
big stallion.

"Ole Dusty was right," he said, dropping his eyes to th
bloody body of Covacs. "That's a tolerable fierce hoss."

Red nodded, pride in his gaze as he looked at his cousi
Dusty Fog, the fastest gun in Texas.

"Sure," Red agreed. "And that's a tolerable fierce m
who tamed him."